Twisted EMPIRE

VIGILANTE KINGS BOOK FOUR

EVA CHANCE
& HARLOW KING

Twisted Empire

Book 4 in the Vigilante Kings series

This is a work of fiction. Any resemblance to actual persons, living or dead, or actual events is purely coincidental.

First Digital Edition, 2022

Cover design: Temptation Creations

Cover photography: CJC Photography, www.cjc-photography.com

Model: Niko Wirachman

Ebook ISBN: 978-1-998752-05-8

Paperback ISBN: 978-1-998752-06-5

CHAPTER
ONE

Madelyn

sat tensed in the backseat of an unfamiliar SUV, staring at the pistol trained directly between my eyes and trying to determine exactly how I'd gotten here. It had happened so quickly—and been so incomprehensible—that I was still having trouble wrapping my head around the apparent facts.

Logan's mother was alive.

Logan's mother was holding a gun to my head, after dragging me away from Logan and the rest of my guys at the strange medical facility we'd been investigating.

I'd only seen the woman next to me in photos from before her supposed death more than ten years ago, but I could recognize the matching curves of her features, the pale hair and dark eyes that were so like Logan's.

And from his response, he'd had no doubt it was her either.

How could she be alive? Where had she been all this time—why had she stayed away?

Why had she appeared out of the blue *now* of all times?

And what did she want with *me*? We'd never even met before.

My gaze dropped to her prosthetic hand resting on the middle seat between us. Logan had told me that he and his father had been forced to bury only her hand. They'd assumed the rest of her body had burned up in the explosion.

But really she'd simply left it behind… to create a convincing story of her death? Why had she wanted to disappear at all?

My mouth opened and closed, but it was hard to summon the courage to ask any of those questions with the gun staring me down.

My phone, which I'd shoved into my hip pocket, chimed with an incoming text. Faster than I would have expected—which maybe was wrong of me, considering how nimble I'd seen Slade move with his mechanical leg —Logan's mom switched the pistol to her prosthetic hand and leaned forward to yank the phone from my pocket. She held down the button to turn it completely off and shoved it into her purse before swapping gun-hands again.

"You won't be talking with anyone else for a good long while," she said.

I glanced at the driver, but all I could see of him was the back of his head with its ruddy buzzcut as he kept the SUV in motion. No sign that he thought there was anything strange about what his passengers were getting up to.

My attention shifted to the window next to me. If I could keep track of where we were going—

But Logan's mom obviously guessed my intentions. She tsked her tongue at me and dug a strip of black fabric out of her purse. "Put this over your eyes," she said, tossing it to me.

When I balked, she waved the gun. "I could start shooting off fingers and see how many you'll be left to work with when you give in."

She sounded totally serious—and totally calm about the threat. A shudder ran down my spine.

My jaw clenching, I grabbed the blindfold and tied it over my eyes. I meant to leave it a little loose with a sliver of visibility at the bottom, but no such luck.

"Tighter," Logan's mom demanded.

I gritted my teeth and tugged the knot a little more. Only a faint glow of light remained at the edge of my vision. I wasn't figuring anything out from that.

"Why are you doing this?" I couldn't help asking, wincing inwardly at how pathetic my quavering voice sounded.

"Don't you worry about that."

Yeah, right. Don't worry about the fact that I was being kidnapped at gunpoint. If I hadn't been so on edge, I'd have rolled my eyes.

This was Logan's mother, the woman who'd raised him for the first ten years of his life. She couldn't be completely horrible, could she? She'd acted like she still cared about him in the few moments before she'd grabbed me.

"Logan thought you were dead," I said cautiously. "Where've you been all this time?"

"That's none of your business. Just sit there quietly and this'll be easier for all of us."

For her, anyway. My heart thumped louder, but I risked another question. "How did you find us at that building?"

Was *she* tangled up in the crimes we'd been investigating somehow?

"Keep *quiet*," Logan's mom snapped. "I'm doing what I need to do to keep my son safe. If he matters at all to you, you'll accept it."

How the hell did kidnapping me keep Logan safe? My mind whirled with confusion, but before I could open my mouth again, the muzzle of the gun tapped my temple.

"Enough," she repeated with a hard edge in her voice, as if she'd predicted what I was thinking.

It wasn't as if she was telling me anything useful anyway. I pressed my lips flat and tried to track the turns and stops of the SUV as it rumbled onward. But at this point, I didn't even know if we were heading into the city or farther away from it.

There was a long, unbroken stretch while the engine

roared, and I suspected we'd gotten on a highway. Apprehension prickled over my skin.

Just how far were we going? Where was she taking me?

And what was she going to do with me there?

I didn't like how much time seemed to pass before the car finally came to a full halt, followed by the click of the parking brake. Logan's mom shifted on the seat next to me with a rustle of her clothes. The door at my other side opened, presumably at the driver's hand, and she prodded me to go out ahead of her.

My feet thudded onto a concrete surface. The air was still and slightly damp around me, and the clang of the closing door echoed off a low ceiling. An underground parking garage?

That didn't really narrow my location down.

"Come along," Logan's mom said, grasping my arm with her prosthetic hand. I let her guide me, adrift in the darkness behind the blindfold.

Hinges squeaked. We stepped onto a carpeted surface and paused there. Then there was a whir like an elevator door opening.

My suspicion was confirmed when the floor beneath our feet started to rise. My stomach flipped over with the rush of its ascent.

From the time it took even without any stops in between, we must have gone up several floors. The car glided to a stop, the door opened with a ping, and Logan's mom hustled me out again.

I lost track of the space we moved through, past

another door, around a corner, my foot bumping into the edge of a piece of furniture. I stumbled, and Logan's mom yanked me upright.

"This way," she snapped, and propelled me onward.

"If you'd let me take off the blindfold—"

"Forget about it."

Another door opened, and she escorted me into a space that felt tighter than the others. Fabric rustled all around us. Logan's mom yanked my arms behind my back.

My instinct was to shove away from her in self-defense, but I had no idea where the gun was now. I had no idea how many other armed people might be nearby. I wasn't in a position to get the upper hand, so I forced myself to remain still while she wrapped what felt like a silk scarf around my wrists, binding them together behind me.

Then she set one hand on my shoulder and pressed down. I sank to my knees, and she backed away.

"I don't want to be bothered by you, so if you scream, I'll knock you out," she said tightly. "Nobody else will hear you here, so it's pointless to even try, but it will be an annoyance."

Her footsteps tapped away, and a door smacked shut. Quiet settled around me.

I was alone.

After a minute of listening, confirming that Logan's mom wasn't immediately coming back, I scooted a little to one side and then another. Fabrics with different textures brushed my face and shoulders. My knee bumped into the pointed toe of a shoe. A picture started to form in my mind.

She'd locked me in a walk-in closet. It was probably about as effective as a prison could get in an ordinary apartment, all the clothing muffling sound from inside.

Had she been telling the truth about there being no one who'd hear me, or had she just been trying to take away my hope?

I needed a better idea of what I was dealing with. Experimenting too aggressively wouldn't be worth it if I ended up unconscious as she'd threatened.

I squirmed around as quietly as I could until I found a bare patch of solid wall. Tipping toward it, I rested the side of my face against the plaster. Then I jerked my head downward.

Again. And again. And again.

The blindfold gradually loosened and slid upward on my face. In a few minutes, I'd lifted it right off my eyes.

I squinted around me in the dark space. I couldn't see a whole lot more than before, but a slit of light showed beneath the door.

I'd been right about it being a walk-in closet. Shirts and pants and dresses hung on hangers on three walls around me. I'd been rubbing my face on the doorframe. Shoes stood in rows beneath the hanging clothes with more on the shelves overhead.

I hadn't heard Logan's mom lock the door, and it'd be pretty unusual for a closet to have a lock on it anyway. But that didn't mean that bursting out into the apartment was a good idea. Her footsteps filtered through the door, moving from one room to another. She was still out there, and who knew who else was with her.

And the gun. That was the biggest problem. I had to play this smart, not run out and get myself into an even worse predicament.

Swiveling around again, I leaned toward the door. If she walked right out of the place, I wanted to know. And it'd be good to figure out if anyone else was in the apartment with her, and if so, how many people there were.

A sudden, heavy thump from somewhere ahead and to my right made my nerves jump. That had sounded like an outer door. Had she left me completely alone already?

Before more than a tiny flicker of hope could light in my chest, a male voice boomed through the space, diffusing it. "What are you doing, Yvonne?"

There was no mistaking the irritation in the man's tone. Footsteps hustled over to him, and Logan's mom —Yvonne, I'd forgotten that was her first name— answered in a rush.

"I was just fixing our little problem, darling. We have leverage now—Logan won't dig any deeper while he's worried about the girl."

The man snorted. "You're creating a new problem, more like it."

Her voice dropped too low for me to make out

whatever she said next. She didn't want me overhearing their conversation.

What I'd already heard had only bewildered me more. Who was she calling *darling* and why did either of them care what Logan had been digging into?

As the man responded in a similarly low voice, I pressed my ear right against the gap by the doorframe. The solid edge bit into my skin, but I could just piece together most of the words when I focused all my attention on them.

"—know my son. It will work." That was Yvonne.

"I can't afford to have a bunch of damn kids messing up my business," the man muttered in return. "I don't care if one of those kids is yours. There are consequences, and you know that."

"They don't have any idea what they're really getting into."

"They should by now. Digging into buried history, sticking their noses where they don't belong—taking up my time when I've got more important things I should be dealing with. I can handle them once and for all, and this will be over."

Yvonne's next response had an almost frantic breathiness to it. "Darling, no. This is enough. I've watched Logan, and I'm positive he won't risk the Silver girl's life over his silly hobby. And she can't do any more harm while we've got her either."

My stomach sank as the pieces clicked together in my head. The only person's business we'd been digging into was the crime lord who'd framed Beckett, the one who was a fellow member of the powerful underground organization Beckett called the Devil's Dozen.

Doom's Seed.

Could that really be *him* out there—the man whose worst crimes we'd gradually been uncovering? The one whose men had tried to massacre Beckett's people just this afternoon?

My stomach knotted. I couldn't think of any other explanation. Who else would have been tracking us so closely and known enough about the situation to realize we'd be at that building today?

And Logan's mother was calling him "darling." Was she *dating* him—the man who'd orchestrated my dad's murder?

How the hell would they even have met?

The man I was increasingly sure was Doom's Seed let out a growl of frustration. "We should kill her and all the others and wash our hands of it. Simple and straight to the point."

A few footsteps rapped toward the closet, and my heart lurched. Yvonne hustled after him.

"No," she said. "You promised—you said once I left him behind, we could leave him alone to live his life."

"Not when the way he's living his life is fucking up my plans. You knew how my world worked when you signed up for this. He's already gotten the second chance you bought for him—it's not my fault he's throwing it away with this stupid quest."

I froze, my pulse skipping a beat. *The second chance you bought for him.*

He couldn't mean…

"He'll never put it all together," Yvonne said pleadingly. "You've covered up the organ routes and the hospital records so well. We'll just hold on to the girl until everyone's thinking straight and realizes just how much is on the line, and everything will be fine."

Doom's Seed let out a huff. "It sounds like you're having second thoughts about your choice to stick with me, Yvonne."

"No. Of course not. I'm doing this *for* you. Less blood on your hands means fewer crimes the police might investigate, doesn't it?"

He paused. "Fine. We'll try your way for a day or two. But if it isn't working out *perfectly*, we end this immediately. It's enough of a mess already."

"It'll work. I swear. Thank you, darling."

Yvonne's voice had turned so simpering it'd have turned my stomach if my gut wasn't already churning with queasiness. The footsteps moved away, and their voices faded again until I couldn't hear them at all.

I slumped down on the floor, my spirits sinking. The weight of what I'd just discovered pressed down on my shoulders.

Organ routes and hospital records. A second chance Logan's mom had bought for him. The operating table in the facility we'd discovered—the pills that corresponded with his transplant medication. We'd wondered what it all meant, the suspicion starting to emerge, but those comments brought the picture completely into focus.

Doom's Seed was harvesting body parts and arranging illegal transplants—and Logan's liver had been one of those illicit organs. I didn't know why his mom would have felt the need to turn to a criminal for help, but every other part of the scenario made far too much sense.

That was how she'd met Doom's Seed in the first place. And that was how my dad could have gotten involved. He'd seen something suspicious in those doctored records and started following the trail from there.

And that was why Doom's Seed had ordered Dad's death… just like he was on the verge of ordering mine and those of the Vigil guys as well.

Had Yvonne faked her death to be with this murderous asshole? What the hell had she been thinking?

I stared at the closet door in a gloomy daze. It didn't really matter why she had. From what I'd heard, she didn't hold anywhere near as much influence over her lover as she wanted to, even when it came to her son. Definitely not when it came to me. She'd barely bought any time at all before he slaughtered us too.

Was I even going to make it out of this apartment to tell the guys what I'd learned?

CHAPTER
TWO

Beckett

"She grabbed her," Logan said, pacing unceasingly as he repeated that part of his story. He raked his hand back through his short chestnut-brown hair. "My mom… she just took her. Held a fucking gun on her and took her."

His voice echoed through the vacant guest house that my family hadn't used in years—a house that shouldn't have any obvious ties to the Storm. It'd been the closest nearby building where the Vigil guys and I could regroup without worrying about the police or Doom's Seed's people finding us.

We needed to find Maddie, and we couldn't worry about anything else in the meantime.

Slade had managed to sit down on one of the

armchairs in the dusty living room, but his knee bounced incessantly, the bright metal ankle of his prosthetic showing when his pantleg swayed. "Your *dead* mom. What the hell is going on here?"

Logan shook his head. "I haven't seen the slightest reason to believe that she was still alive in the last eleven years. I never would have thought she'd leave us on purpose. I had no idea she was even capable of handling a gun. Damn it." He aimed a kick at the baseboard, hard enough that it probably hurt his toes.

Dexter had been staring off into space as if processing everything from a distance, his normally alert green eyes gone hazy. Now, he glanced Logan's way. "Are you sure it was your mom who came and grabbed Madelyn? It wasn't just someone who looked like your mother?"

"It was her. One hundred percent. The way she talked to me..." Logan let out a ragged breath. "She told me she was *proud* of me, for fuck's sake, and then she yanked Maddie away from me. She told me I had to stop digging—she's got to be involved with the people we're investigating somehow. It doesn't make sense!"

"We'll figure it out," I said, reaching for my phone. "Whatever else is going on, I'll get my best people tracking that car. We'll figure out where your mother took Maddie and get her back. Maybe Lindell will cough up some more information too."

I didn't have a lot of hope about that last possibility. We'd dropped off the local lieutenant who answered to Doom's Seed with a bunch of my people so they could interrogate him at length. He'd have been too much baggage to drag around with us while we searched for Maddie. And I had the feeling he'd already coughed up as much as he'd be willing to—he'd choose death before saying more.

"Maddie still had her phone on her, right?" I said to Logan as I tapped my phone's screen.

He nodded, and just a tiny bit of the tension wound tight inside me released. That was a reason to hope.

Of course, who knew what this woman who seemed to have risen from the dead had already done to Maddie? What her goals were? Why she'd intervened at all?

This whole situation had gotten far more complicated than I liked, and I had no idea how to untangle it when new snags rose up faster than we could work through the previous ones.

My jaw clenched, but I forced my voice to stay even when my main tech guy on staff picked up. "I have a phone number I need you to trace," I said. "And I also need you to check the traffic cams around that address you sent me to earlier today for a black SUV. Follow its route as well as you can and figure out where it's gone."

"No problem, boss," Luis replied without hesitation.

I set the phone on my lap, my fingers curling tight around it as I looked around at the other guys. Until recently, they'd seen my criminal connections as reason to distrust me. Would they blame me for how the violence we were facing had escalated—claim it was *my* fault that Maddie had ended up at the wrong end of a gun?

My stomach twisted at the thought. I didn't know how this would work if we ended up divided again, whether I could ensure her safety alone.

The best thing I could do was show that I was working as hard as possible to get Maddie out of danger right now.

I focused on Logan. "Do you know any places around here where your mom could have gone to hide out—old properties, family friends, favorite spots to visit…?"

Logan shook his head and then pressed the heels of his hands against his temples. "Not that I can think of. But, I mean, I obviously don't know anything about this woman at all."

"Did she have any close friends who faded out of your family's life after she supposedly died?"

He paused and then groaned. "I don't know. I didn't pay that much attention to my parents' social lives."

Dexter frowned, his dark curls tumbling across his forehead as he tilted his head. "We could try searching property and rental listings for her name—but she must have been using a fake name and IDs once her death was registered."

"Yeah, that won't get us anywhere." Slade swiped his hand across his mouth and then looked at me. "Can you talk to Doom's Seed? Take him to task for this war he—or Lindell—started against you and find out if he knows anything about Maddie getting kidnapped? Everything seems to lead back to him."

It did, which didn't reassure me at all. I gritted my teeth as I considered my options.

"There are specific channels of communication I have to use to reach out to him," I admitted. "I can't just call him up—I wouldn't know how. And he could take hours or even days to respond if he decides to. He wasn't very cooperative before. We don't have that kind of time. And even if we did, the chances that he'd tell me anything helpful are next to none." I paused. "I'm not sure it'd be a good thing for him to realize how much Maddie's disappearance matters to me."

"Okay, you have a point there." Slade sighed and sagged back in the chair. The color had leached from his normally warm brown skin.

I swallowed hard, my throat constricting with my expanding sense of failure, and my phone pinged with an incoming text from Luis. I lifted the device and immediately grimaced.

"My main tech guy can't trace Maddie's phone," I said. "At best, it's shut off. At worst, it's been destroyed. And there were no traffic cams near the medical facility. He's running a wider search for a black SUV in the right timeframe, but it's hard to pick up when we don't even have the license plate."

Logan swore. "My mom must know what she's doing—or someone helping her does. How could she...?" He let out a strangled sound of frustration.

"Hold on," I said, flicking through my contacts.

"My tech people are good, but they're not the absolute best out there. If there are any new tricks or techniques, I know at least one guy who might be a bit more in the know."

I dialed Gideon's number, but the call went straight to voicemail, not even ringing once. My muscles tensed further as I tried the rest of the Paradise Bend crew: Rowan and Wylder, Kaige and even Mercy. The result was the same.

They must have been in the middle of a deal or some other work where they couldn't be disturbed. There was no telling when they'd be available again either.

And it'd been a long shot anyway. Gideon was brilliant, but his actual experience was mainly on his home turf, not on the level of groups like the Devil's Dozen. I wasn't totally sure he'd have been able to outdo my own people when searching territory he wasn't familiar with.

As that thought passed through my mind, inspiration hit me with a jolt. The possibility felt even more tenuous than my connection to Gideon, but if it worked out…

I sat up straighter, and the other guys immediately focused on me even more intently.

"What?" Logan demanded.

I wet my lips. "There's another member of the Devil's Dozen I could reach out to who I think is more likely to get back to me quickly if I say it's urgent. Our newest member—she took out the man who used to hold the spot, and since then she's been disbanding a lot of his more unsavory business as if she doesn't agree with them. It seems like she has a more solid moral compass than most of my colleagues."

Slade perked up, flicking his dark brown hair away from his eyes as he peered at me. "And she'd know how to track down Logan's mom and Maddie?"

"I'm not sure," I admitted. "But I've heard murmurs that her closest associates are highly skilled mercenaries, so *they* should be the kind of people who know how to locate a target… It's far from a guarantee, but I can't think of anyone else to call on."

I braced myself for them to hesitate or even berate me for suggesting this course of action—for wanting to draw another high-level criminal into our problems with unknown consequences. How much did they even trust my judgment about who we could rely on?

But in a matter of seconds, all three of the Vigil guys were nodding.

"We have to take every available option," Dexter said.

Logan motioned to my phone. "What are you waiting for? Make that call!"

In spite of everything, a tiny spark of warmth lit in the midst of the turmoil gripping my chest. They were counting on me, cooperating with me. Working with me rather than shutting me out like I was another enemy, the way they had before. They recognized that I knew how to navigate the dark underworld we'd entered better than the rest of them, and they accepted it.

We might have had our disagreements in the past, but we were united by the belief that we needed to protect Maddie at all costs.

I tapped Lana's name on my phone's screen. If anyone could find the fastest way to send a message to another Devil's Dozen member, it was the Storm's business manager.

"It looks like you got the immediate disaster under control," she said without preamble when she picked up. "Impressive work there."

"Thank you," I said automatically. It was hard to think about the assault my people had faced that Maddie had been so instrumental in overcoming when now Maddie's life was on the line. "I have another disaster in progress… and I'd like to speak to the Blood Hunter about it as soon as possible. Can you pull all the strings you have access to and see if you can make that happen?"

Lana hadn't gotten her position by questioning the people in charge. "On it," she said without missing a beat, and ended the call.

"I don't know how long it'll take," I told the guys as I set the phone aside again. "Let's see if we can make any more progress on our own in the meantime." My own people might still get us somewhere. I focused on Logan. "Can you remember any details about the SUV your mom was traveling in? Something that could help pick it out of all the other black SUVs out there?"

Logan made a face. "I was so fucking distracted. If I'd just reacted fast enough to check the license plate…"

His brawny shoulders tensed with frustration. "Details… It looked very new. Totally clean, really shiny. Almost definitely a recent model. That's the only thing that stood out about it, at least that I noticed."

"That helps." I wrote out a text to Luis. "Did you see what model it was, or even the make?"

"No. God damn it."

I looked up from my phone, my mouth twisting into a pained but sympathetic smile. "It isn't your fault. The mom you believed was dead was standing right there in front of you. Of course you weren't worrying about the car."

"None of us would have paid much attention in a situation like that," Dexter put in.

Logan glanced at him. "I wish you'd been out there snapping your pictures." Then his head lifted higher. "You were taking pictures inside the place. We should go over those—maybe we'll see a clue that connects to my mom that we missed while we were there."

"It's worth a shot." Slade pulled out his phone. "Have you got them in the cloud yet, Dex?"

"Adding them now." Dexter paused and then caught my gaze in one of his fleeting moments of eye contact. "I can add you to the album too."

That offer brought a hint of a real smile to my face. "That'd be great. I want to do everything I can—and the more eyes the better, right?"

After a half hour of scanning the photos, zooming in and peering at every nook and cranny, my spirits were starting to sink. None of us had turned up anything so far, and there weren't many pictures left to study—and at least one of the other guys had already looked at anything I hadn't.

I was just sucking in my breath, trying to figure out what to suggest we do next, when my phone's ringtone pealed out.

I snatched up the phone and yanked it to my ear at the sight of the call display. "Lana, what have you got for me?"

Her professional satisfaction hummed through her voice. "The Blood Hunter is willing to speak to you immediately. Should I connect you now?"

My heart skipped a beat. I hit the speaker button and set my phone on the coffee table between the four of us so we could all be included in the conversation.

"Absolutely," I said. "I can't wait to speak to her."

CHAPTER
THREE

Madelyn

shifted my arms up and down, stretching the silky material binding my wrists so it gradually loosened. I'd been working at it on and off for what felt like hours, and every time I felt a little more give.

The smooth fabric didn't hold a knot well. I got the impression Yvonne didn't have a whole lot of experience at restraining prisoners. Lucky for me.

She'd left me alone in the walk-in closet the entire time. After Doom's Seed had marched out again, I hadn't heard any voices, only a single set of footsteps occasionally pattering from one room to another. At this point, I was sure it was just the two of us in the apartment.

How long that would last, it was impossible to guess.

I squirmed my arms a little more and tested my compressed hand against the binding. This time, the loop of fabric finally slid over the base of my thumb.

My heart skipped a beat. If I wanted to, I could slide my bindings right off now. I'd be free.

Other than the closet door and the woman with the gun waiting between me and the outside world.

I sank onto my butt to rest for a moment and consider my options. I could have called Yvonne's bluff and yelled for help, but even if *she* would have risked someone hearing me, I couldn't believe a huge crime boss like Doom's Seed would have let her keep me here if there were people nearby who'd hear a loud shout.

I couldn't count on anyone coming to help me. My guys wouldn't have any idea where she'd taken me.

To get out of this mess, I could only count on myself.

I had two tools at my disposal: persuasion and force. I wasn't sure either would be enough, but starting with the one less likely to get me killed seemed like the best idea.

First I wanted to scope out as much of my surroundings as I could and see if I could add any tools to my limited arsenal.

I pressed my face against the doorframe and used the friction to tug the blindfold back over my eyes, so she wouldn't realize I'd been able to dislodge it. Leaving my hands in their silky restraint, I scooted a little back from the door.

"Hey!" I hollered. "Are you still there? I need to use the bathroom. Unless you want me to pee in here on your stuff."

Yvonne's footsteps quickly tapped across the floor to the closet. It'd obviously been long enough that she could believe I genuinely needed to go—and I did feel a real twinge in my bladder.

The door clicked open. "Come on, then," Yvonne said brusquely, grasping the side of my arm to tug me to my feet. "Let's be quick about it."

I couldn't make out anything other than the hardwood floor as she escorted me down a hall and into a tiled bathroom. The boards in the hall gleamed with polish, not a mark on them—like they'd recently been laid down. That didn't help me with my escape, though.

Yvonne followed me right into the bathroom. "Can I get a little privacy?" I protested as she loosened my jeans.

"I'm making sure you don't get up to anything you shouldn't. You don't have anything I haven't seen before."

I had to restrain a flinch as her cool hands dragged my jeans and panties down my thighs. She pushed me down on the toilet, an awkward fit with my arms bound behind me. I forced my pelvis to relax so I could actually go and keep up my story, my skin itching with mortification.

So much for searching the place. She wasn't giving

me a second alone to take a peek at my surroundings or grab anything. What I wouldn't have given for something as simple as a pair of nail scissors…

But there was no point in moping about the impossible.

"I'm done," I said when I was sure nothing more would come out.

"Then stand up. I'm not wiping you."

I guessed I'd rather that than have her reach right between my legs. Even the thought made me shudder.

I got to my feet, and she yanked up my jeans. She was using two hands, I noted, which meant she wasn't holding her gun right now. But she probably had it in her pocket within easy reach. I didn't like my odds of getting out of my bindings and making it to the door before she was ready to shoot me.

Not while she was still so alert, anyway.

Time to give persuasion a try.

As Yvonne hustled me back to the closet, I couldn't help wishing I'd managed to absorb more of Slade's easy charm. I was good with facts and problem-solving, not so much with cajoling people into getting my way.

Maybe I should start by getting some facts, then. See if I could understand how both of us had ended up in this awful situation.

"Why are you doing this to me?" I asked as she pushed me ahead of her into the closet. My shoulder brushed the hanging shirts and dresses. "You know that Logan cares about me. You know how upset he'll be if something happens to me. He'll never forgive you."

"Then you'd better behave so that it doesn't come to that."

"You're really going to let me go at some point? That's not how stories like this usually end, and I think you know that." I didn't want to let on that I'd overheard Doom's Seed's threats, but she had to realize the likely outcome was obvious.

Yvonne simply let out a huff but didn't answer. I pressed harder. "Don't you care about your son at all?"

Yvonne prodded me farther into the closet. My back hit the clothes along the far wall with a jangling of the hangers. I half expected her to storm off, but she stayed in place. I could sense her standing there a few feet away —not close enough for me to reach her, but not leaving either.

"You have no idea what you're talking about," she said with a rasp in her voice. "You're practically a kid still. I already gave up *everything* for Logan. You'd never comprehend what I've been through or the choices I've needed to make."

My stomach twisted at her tone. "Did you have to run off and fake your death? Whoever you're with now, that man who came in earlier—did he force you?"

Yvonne let out a cool laugh. "That was my one consolation prize after everything else fell apart. You don't know what real love is yet either, even if you imagine you do."

She figured she was in love with a murderous criminal overlord, then? I restrained a shiver. No, I definitely couldn't comprehend that at all. He obviously wasn't even trying to put on a show of having a conscience, talking about killing me and her own son for nothing more than trying to get at the truth.

"You could have stayed with Logan," I couldn't help pointing out. "You didn't *have* to leave him."

"I made the best choices I had with the hand I was dealt."

Her shoes squeaked against the floor as if she were turning to go. I wasn't getting anywhere by talking to her.

My pulse stuttered, but I knew what I had to do, even if the thought made me queasy. If I couldn't convince her to sympathize with me using my words, I'd have to turn to my fists.

And to accomplish that, I needed her on this side of the closet door. Preferably as close to me as possible.

"So you're a shitty mother, basically," I tossed out. "Putting your love life over being there for your son. Some sacrifice."

As I spoke, I flexed my arms and felt the give of the silk scarf. I could slip my hands out in an instant—as soon as it was the *right* instant.

Yvonne whirled back around with a rustle of her clothes. "Don't you *dare* make any judgments about my choices when you haven't got a clue what you're talking about."

"Oh, I think I have a pretty good idea," I said, putting on as caustic a tone as I could manage. A little honest anger bubbled up inside me at the memories of Logan mourning the woman in front of me. "You met this guy, and you had an inconvenient husband you weren't quite as head over heels for anymore, so you chucked your whole family in the trash to chase your new 'love.'"

"It wasn't like that," Yvonne snapped. "Shut up about things you don't understand."

"I understand how much it hurt both Holand and Logan, losing you. I've seen the pain on their faces, over and over. You'd know how much losing you wrecked them if you'd bothered to pay any attention instead of only caring about yourself."

"I did what I had to do. Shut your mouth and mind your own business."

I forced a derisive snort. "You kidnapped me. I think it's one hundred percent my business that you're a selfish, conniving bitch who never gave a damn about anyone other than—"

My taunts jabbed deep enough that Yvonne didn't even let me finish my sentence. She strode forward and slapped me across the face hard enough that my head jerked to the side, my cheek stinging.

But that was exactly what I'd wanted.

Even as her palm collided with my cheekbone, I was shoving my wrists free from the scarf.

My hands whipped forward, one snatching off the blindfold, the other already aiming a punch where I'd been able to estimate her head was. My knuckles slammed into her temple, just a tad off course. I'd hoped to sock her in the nose.

Yvonne shrieked as she stumbled to the side. She

groped at her hip, no doubt for the gun, but I rushed at her with all of my strength and every instinct my Krav Maga training had drilled into me.

I just had to keep hitting until I was sure I could get away.

I kept my fists flying and swiped out with my foot as well. Yvonne flailed at me, curling her fingers into claws and stabbing her elbow at me, but it was obvious she had no training at all. I managed to dodge her blows and then kicked at her ankles, making her stagger.

At the last second, she managed to head-butt me in the stomach. I let out a whoomph as the air left my lungs, but then I flung myself forward again.

When I rammed my heel into her knee, she buckled over. I grabbed her hair at the back of her head and smacked her face down into the floor with all my might.

Yvonne groaned, her body trembling with the impact. She sagged to the side in a daze, and I sprang past her out the closet door.

Yanking it shut behind me, I scanned the room for something to hold it closed. An oak desk stood against the wall right next to the closet. When I shoved it over, I found it was as heavy as I'd hoped.

I hefted it in front of the closet and then dashed out of the bedroom.

Yvonne's furious voice rang out behind me as she started to pummel the door from inside the closet. "Get back here, you bitch! Let me out, or you'll wish I *had* killed you in the first place."

Ignoring her threats, I dashed through the

apartment's living room. My gaze caught on a purse I recognized as Yvonne's from the first moments in the car—the purse she'd stuffed my phone in. Without slowing down, I caught hold of the straps and yanked it off the sofa.

I spared a quick glance out the living room window, but I couldn't see anything in the dark except the glow of city lights through the night that had fallen while I was trapped. My stomach flipped over.

It'd definitely been hours. The guys would be frantic.

I darted out the front door. The second it slammed behind me, Yvonne's screeches faded away. I sprinted toward the elevator—and jerked to a stop when I saw the floor number on the digital display creeping upward.

Someone was riding up. Maybe to another floor—or maybe it was Doom's Seed's people or the man himself coming straight here.

Shit. I dove into the stairwell at the end of the hall instead. My shoes thundered over the stairs as I dashed down them as fast as my feet would fly.

I'd won my freedom, and I was not letting myself get caught again.

CHAPTER
FOUR

Dexter

I t was hard to feel hopeful about Madelyn's fate when all we had was a cell phone and a blank-screened laptop sitting next to each other on the coffee table. But the woman Beckett referred to as "the Blood Hunter" was talking on speakerphone while the voice of one of her associates carried from the laptop, and apparently he had significant technological skills.

He didn't appear to be all that keen on using those skills to help us, though. "Who exactly is this woman you're trying to track down?" he asked with a note of suspicion in his voice.

Beckett leaned toward the devices on the table, his pale hair drifting across his forehead as his gray eyes turned even more intense. "She's my girlfriend. Who was kidnapped, probably at least in part *because* she's my girlfriend."

"And I can assume you're telling the truth because…?"

There was a rustling sound, and I got the impression the Blood Hunter had swatted him. "This is the Storm's heir—the one I told you seems like he's open to changing some things in the Devil's Dozen. I wouldn't have suggested we do this if I didn't believe his story."

"All right, all right," the man said in a tone that had quickly turned teasing. "You're the boss. Why don't you have a tech genius of your own, Mr. Heir of the Storm?"

"I do," Beckett said dryly. "But it turns out he's not quite brilliant enough. Your 'boss' seems to think you might be able to top him."

"Oh, probably." The man on the other end tsked his tongue. "No phone signal to track, and no way to trace the kidnapping vehicle?"

"Exactly."

Logan leaned forward from where we were all poised around the coffee table, his broad hands flexing and clenching. I was sitting rigidly still, but his obvious edginess resonated with the tension winding through my body.

We *had* to find Madelyn. How could we have lost her—and like this? Logan's mom still alive, taking her hostage…

I wasn't sure how she *or* Logan were going to be okay after this.

"Are you going to show us what you're doing?"

Logan demanded. "All we can see is a black screen so far."

"Don't worry, we're all linked up. There's just nothing to show yet."

"So, you *are* going to show us something at some point?" Slade asked, his casual tone a little more terse than usual. His dark brown eyes held a glint that looked more dangerous than amused. He was just as worried as the rest of us, even if he was better at hiding it.

"I'm getting to that," the hacker said. "All in good time. Give me her number."

As Beckett rattled it off, I frowned. "But there's no way to track her phone right now."

The man chuckled. "Ah, that's where you're mistaken—and where the Storm's tech guy failed. Someone *really* in the know would be aware that a lot of cellular companies have started adding a function to their firmware that allows you to turn a phone on remotely."

"It's not their fault they don't have access to all the same info you do," the Blood Hunter put in.

"I'm just stating facts."

"You could be a little less patronizing about it."

"All part of my charm." I could practically hear the grin in the man's voice, and my own hands clenched. I didn't want him to be joking around right now—I wanted him to find Madelyn already.

Logan obviously felt similarly. "Great," he said brusquely. "And you can activate this firmware function?"

"Yep! To be fair, very few people are aware this exists. It's high-level law enforcement agencies pushing for the option, but the privacy violation makes it a major legal gray area. Thankfully, I don't really give a shit about legalities."

"Comes with the territory," Beckett remarked.

A little curiosity had lit Logan's gaze despite his frustration. "How exactly does it work?"

If he could still wonder about the technological side even with everything going on, maybe he'd come out of this all right after all.

"I've got to keep a few secrets to myself," the man said as a faint tapping sound carried through the speakers. "Basically, I need to follow the data trail attached to your gal's phone number to track down the activation code that goes with it. Then it's like flicking a switch… except a lot more code-y."

I shifted on my chair with a restlessness I couldn't shake. "How long will you need for that?"

"As long as it takes," the man said, very unhelpfully.

As we waited in uneasy silence, Logan squeezed his knuckles. Beckett got up and poured us all glasses of water from the sink, whether because he was worried about us getting dehydrated or just for something to do with himself, I wasn't sure. Slade gave him a grateful nod. I took a sip from mine and set it down.

We still weren't getting anywhere. What if Madelyn's phone was outright broken, or—

"Got it!" the man crowed on the other end of the line. "Okay, now I need to home in on the signal, and when I've got a clear location, I'll send it to your screen." He paused. "You do realize that this kind of tracking via cell tower never gives an exact address, right? We're going to be looking at a range rather than a specific spot."

Logan had already scooted forward to peer at the laptop. "Of course."

Several more seconds slipped by with the thumping of my pulse, and then an image formed on the screen. A map, contracting to show a smaller area even as its lines became clearer. In less than a minute, we were looking at a square of four city blocks.

Logan tapped at something with the trackpad. "That's about an hour from here." He pushed to his feet.

"But there are a couple dozen buildings in that section of the city," Beckett said. "We can't go bursting into all of them hollering her name and hope that'll work out."

The man hummed to himself. "Unfortunately, that's the best I can narrow it down from the phone. If you can think of other factors that would come into play, I can do my best to account for those too. I'm assuming to hold a kidnapping victim, it'd probably be a place that's not very busy, ideally not open to the public."

My mind started to whirl with possibilities, the gnawing panic fading now that I had a concrete puzzle in front of me. I hadn't been able to help much before, but fitting pieces together—that was *my* expertise.

"The kidnapper wouldn't have wanted to walk her across a public sidewalk with a gun on her," I said. "It'll probably be a building with a secluded parking lot, out of view around back or underground."

"That makes sense." The man clicked something, and several of the buildings on the screen grayed out.

My thoughts raced on, exhilarated by our progress. "There'd need to be a lot of space between where they're holding Madelyn and anyplace bystanders would be nearby, to make sure if she shouted for help no one could hear her. So that would eliminate any of the smaller buildings that are open to the public, I think. At least those that don't have basements."

A few more buildings grayed out, but not enough. I drummed my fingers on the edge of the coffee table, and inspiration sparked.

"Are any of those buildings not open at *all* yet? Not quite finished construction or closed for renovations—someplace they could ensure there'd be no chance of anyone seeing or hearing her?" Our enemies didn't have to be going to those lengths, but if they *could* be that careful, why wouldn't they?

The man let out a low whistle. "You know what, I think you're on to something. There is one condo building here that's finished construction but not yet officially open—no one's moved in. At least not in the existing records."

Beckett stepped forward, his eyes lighting up. "I bet that's where she's been taken."

I didn't want us to go rushing in without total confirmation, though.

"That one building—if no one's living there yet, it

wouldn't be drawing any utilities, right? Can you check whether electricity, water, and heating have been active today?"

"I absolutely can. Ah, ha! All three have been drawn on as recently as this evening. Sneaky, but not quite sneaky enough to defeat the great Blaze."

"You know you just gave them your name, don't you?" the Blood Hunter broke in with amusement lacing her voice.

"Hey, it's an alias anyway. And they do seem like okay people. What do you guys think? Ready to track down your woman?"

Beckett was tucking a pistol into a holster at his waist. "I'd say so. Thank you for your help—and Blood Hunter, don't hesitate to call on the Storm if you feel we can return the favor."

"Never hurts to have an extra ally in my back pocket," she said, and both of the lines cut out.

Slade and I stood up in unison. We hustled with Logan toward the door as Beckett followed behind us, already placing a new call on his phone. "Yeah, I need you at this spot as quickly as you can get there. I'm going to need reinforcements." He recited the address we'd learned as he pulled out his key fob to unlock the doors on his van.

Slade glanced over at me as we clambered into the back, a sense of urgency vibrating through the air. He let out a strained laugh. "Never thought I'd see the day when I'd be racing off with a criminal overlord to rescue the woman I love."

Neither did I, I thought, so automatically that the truth of that statement only fully hit me a second later, with the lurch of the van surging toward the road.

It *was* true, wasn't it? This wrenching pain in my chest, and the frantic need to know Madelyn was okay. The chill that stabbed through me at the thought that she might have been hurt—the rush of relief when I imagined pulling her away from whatever Logan's mom had dragged her into.

I'd never worried about anyone like this before. I'd never wanted to protect someone so badly. A thrill shivered through me with the recognition of how much Madelyn meant to me, but it came with a terrifying flipside.

For the first time in my life, I could say that I loved someone—and if we didn't act quickly enough, I might lose her before I ever got a chance to tell her that.

Madelyn

The stairs rushed by beneath me so quickly that I knew if I tried to think about it too hard, I'd stumble. So I just let my feet fly on, focused only on reaching the bottom. On making it all the way to the door.

When I hit the bottom of the staircase, my breath coming short, I eased more carefully to the windowed door. The dark lobby beyond looked totally empty, no one in the security booth near the front entrance. A few pieces of paper were tacked to the walls, like the kinds of information sheets you'd find in a building under construction.

Was this building even really open yet?

No one arrived in the brief time I was watching, and I knew I couldn't afford to linger very long. If Doom's Seed's people had been going up to Yvonne's apartment in the elevator, they'd have found her trapped in the closet by now.

I pushed out into the lobby and darted across the thickly carpeted floor. At the main door, I glanced around quickly and, seeing only a few cars cruising by under the glow of the streetlamps, slipped out. I strode away from the building as quickly as I could while trying to give the appearance that I was simply in a hurry and not fleeing for my life.

My phone—where was my phone? I had to call the guys—I had to have it in my hand so I could dial 9-1-1 if a bunch of criminals came after me.

I groped inside Yvonne's purse, the contents rattling around my fumbling fingers. But just as I caught hold of what felt like my phone's case, a familiar white van roared around a corner just a couple blocks ahead and raced toward me.

In the first second, I froze, my legs tensing to propel me in the opposite direction in case this was some kind of threat. There was nothing to say Doom's Seed couldn't use white vans too. But before I could dash off, an even more familiar face appeared through the open passenger window.

"Maddie!" Logan called out, his voice ragged.

I bolted toward them rather than away. The van screeched to a halt by the curb with Beckett's face, unusually frantic, staring at me from behind the wheel. Slade and Dexter spilled out of the back, Slade grabbing my arm.

"I'm so glad we found you," he said, yanking me into a swift hug before dragging me toward the van. "Come on. I have the feeling we'd better get out of here fast, yeah?"

"Yeah," I said shakily. "I think that would be a good idea."

I clambered into the back after the guys and dropped into one of the benches against the wall. As Beckett gunned the engine again, Logan twisted in his seat to peer at me. His eyes narrowed.

"Your cheek is bruising. Who the fuck did that to you?"

The protective growl of his voice sent a welcome shiver through me, but the thought of answering him made my stomach clench up.

"Your mom," I admitted.

He winced, his mouth tightening.

"I take it you got away from her," Beckett said, shooting me a quick smile of relief over his shoulder. "You always manage to impress me even after I think I know what you're capable of."

"I had no idea if you guys would even be able to find me," I said. "It didn't seem like I had much choice if I wanted to get out of there. But I'm glad you'd already figured it out. You have no idea how happy I am to see all of you."

"Take a little while to rest and recover while we get you to someplace safe."

"Where can we go that *is* safe?" Dexter asked, shooting me a worried look before focusing on Beckett. "Doom's Seed is obviously still after you and out for blood, and the police are probably continuing to look for the three of us thanks to whatever tip he gave them."

Beckett paused for long enough that my stomach started to sink. Then he shook his head sharply as if arguing with himself.

"I can take you to my main family home," he said. "It's not far, and Doom's Seed wouldn't dare attack us there. We have plenty of security if he wants to try."

Slade's mouth slanted at an uneasy angle. "Are you sure that's a good idea?"

Beckett shrugged. "It's the best place I can offer. I think our lives are so entangled at this point that it won't make anything more difficult for any of us."

"It's fine," Logan said. "Let's just get there."

Beckett pressed on the gas, and the engine revved louder. He reached to tap on his phone. "Everyone can head back to their previous positions now," he said to whoever he'd contacted via speakerphone. "The situation we needed to tackle is resolved for the moment."

Dexter scooted closer to me and tucked his hand around my elbow as he looked me over. It was a small physical gesture, but one that meant a lot from the normally awkward guy. His gaze lingered on my sore cheek for a moment. "Are you hurt anywhere else?"

I touched my stomach cautiously and found it was only a little tender from when Yvonne had slammed her head into my gut. "Nothing serious. It was just… kind of terrifying."

Slade wrapped his arm around my back from my other side and tipped his head against mine. "No kidding. But you're out now. We're not letting *anyone* get their hands on you again."

Logan was still staring back at us, looking like he wanted to climb right between the seats to join the group embrace. "I don't care that she's my mother," he said with an air of menace I'd only heard him use when speaking to or about someone who'd hurt me. "She isn't getting away with this."

My head was spinning with everything I'd learned that I didn't know how to explain, but I knew I had to tell them all one thing before they made any more plans. "She's been working with Doom's Seed. At least, I'm pretty sure it was him, from the things I overheard. That's why she wanted to stop us from investigating."

Logan's forehead furrowed. "How the hell did she end up mixed up with him?"

Oh, God, how did I explain *that* to him? All the pieces that intersected with his life in far too painful ways.

My mouth opened and closed, my throat drying up. "I—I don't know all the details—"

"Hey," Slade interrupted, squeezing me to his side. "Let's give her a chance to recover before we start some kind of interrogation."

Dexter peered at me with his sharp green eyes. "You didn't find out anything that we'd need to deal with right away, did you?"

I shook my head. "No. None of it was urgent, except, well, the kidnapping. Doom's Seed wanted to kill me."

As I said the words, Beckett sucked a rough breath through his teeth. A chill swept through me, the knowledge sinking in even clearer than before of how close I'd come to dying in that apartment.

"That fucking bastard," Logan muttered ominously, his hands flexing.

The van turned down a private driveway, and a heavy wrought-iron gate opened to admit us. "He won't get anywhere near Maddie while she's in here," Beckett said firmly. "Welcome to my home."

I turned to peek out the window, and then I could only stare. We drove through a carefully landscaped yard to a massive three-story house that really could only be called a mansion, Victorian-style in light gray brick with a darker gray trim. It had to be at least four times the size of the house I'd grown up in, surrounded by sweeping lawns and stately trees.

Slade let out a low whistle. "Well, I can't claim that crime doesn't pay."

Beckett parked in a sprawling garage off to the side of the house. The second I eased out of the van, all four guys stepped close around me as if in an unspoken agreement to play bodyguards.

Beckett led the way through a door in the garage

and into a hall that was all dark wood paneling and gilded wallpaper. Our feet padded across a thick rug that stretched the length of the space to an expansive staircase.

"We won't want to disturb my father, but he mostly keeps to his favorite rooms," Beckett said quietly as we headed up the stairs. "I have a few rooms devoted to my use—a sitting area, an office, and a bedroom—all connected kind of like an apartment within the house. There are a few guest bedrooms just down the hall from that as well, so you'll all be able to crash for the night in comfort."

"Comfort?" Slade murmured. "More like total luxury." He stroked his hand up and down my side where he still had his arm around me.

Dexter's grasp had slid from my elbow to my hand. His fingers twined with mine as we stepped through a doorway after Beckett and found ourselves in a room as big as their open concept living-dining room in their apartment, with two linen sofas and a few matching wing chairs in a broad semi-circle around a gas fireplace, an eight-seater mahogany table off to the side, and several bookcases with glass doors. At Beckett's flick of a switch, light beamed down from a crystal chandelier overhead.

He turned toward me, his gaze searching mine. But even as he stepped to meet me with his hand rising as if to run over my hair, Logan pushed in first.

My stepbrother cupped my jaw and pulled me straight into a kiss, heedless of the other guys around us.

His mouth crashed into mine, and all my senses sparked to life. He was kissing me as if his life depended on our embrace, and in that moment, I needed his passion just as much.

I was here. I was okay. I was with the men I loved, and they were going to do whatever they could to ensure I was never in that much danger again.

As much as I'd let them protect me, anyway.

My knees wobbled with the rush of giddying heat. Logan pulled back just an inch, his forehead grazing mine.

"I'm never letting anyone get their hands on you again," he swore. "I don't care who the assholes are who're trying. You belong with me. With *us*."

He glanced around at the other three guys, and their combined attention seared over my skin with twice as much heat as Logan's kiss had generated.

Beckett reached past him to guide my lips toward his. He claimed my mouth with a similar passion but plenty of tenderness as well. It felt like a statement of ownership and an apology wrapped into one.

It was one of *his* enemies who'd threatened me. Even if my own actions had drawn that man's attention to me, I didn't think Beckett would ever absolve himself of blame. "Never again," he said hoarsely when he drew back.

Slade leaned in to press his lips to my temple, his fingers teasing up under the hem of my shirt now. "No one will take you away from us again. If Logan isn't in a position to make sure of that, I will."

"And if neither of them can, I'll be here." Dexter raised his other hand to trace his index finger along my jaw, the mix of anguish and desire in his normally calm expression making my heart stutter.

"Just as long as you're okay with me protecting you too, when I can," I had to say.

Beckett let out a dismissive huff. "If I have my way, it won't be required in either direction very soon. But for just a little while, I think we can focus on showing you just how much we missed you."

His mouth caught mine again, melding with my lips before flicking his tongue between them. As it tangled with my own tongue, one of Slade's hands wound in my hair to massage my scalp with his dexterous fingers. I leaned my weight into him while Beckett messed with the bottom of my shirt, slipping it barely past my lower stomach before pausing.

He gripped my bare skin with his warm hands and took a deep breath to control himself. Slade leaned forward, resting his lips at the place where my neck met my shoulders and planting warm kisses there. Dexter took the initiative to ease my face toward him so he could draw me into a kiss himself.

I kissed him back hard, wanting him to know he meant just as much to me as the other guys even if he wasn't as confident. When my hand clutched at his shirt, he made a breathless sound against my mouth and pushed even closer against me.

Logan towered over us all, caressing a slow path

along the waist of my jeans. In a matter of seconds, my panties were soaked. I couldn't restrain a needy whimper.

Beckett gripped my waist and tugged me toward one of the room's other doorways. "I think we should take this to the bedroom. Now."

Logan reached for me, but to my surprise, Dexter slipped his arms around me first. In a gesture I'd have expected from any of the other guys before him, he swept me right off my feet to cradle me against his lean but toned chest.

Slade let out an approving chuckle, and a sly smile crossed Logan's face, seeing his friend's growing assurance. We moved together to the bedroom door, my panties fully drenched now as I tucked my head against Dexter's neck.

When we stepped into Beckett's bedroom, the crisply masculine scent of him flooded my nose, making my mouth water. The pale blue walls, impeccably tidy dresser and side tables, and massive four-poster bed all fit the man I knew perfectly.

Dexter strode straight to the bed. One of the other guys might have tossed me onto it, but he had his own approach. He stood over the mattress and bent carefully to set me on the soft comforter like I was a precious artifact.

Then he climbed over me and sought out my lips. The heat of his mouth capturing mine washed through my entire body, leaving my skin tingling as if he were touching me everywhere through that one point of contact.

The other guys were climbing onto the bed around us. Someone's hand teased up my inner thigh to stroke between my legs. Another set of fingers tugged up my shirt. I was burning up all over, squirming with need. How was I ever going to survive all four of these incredible men at once?

I wasn't sure, but I was absolutely looking forward to finding out.

As I fumbled with the button on Dexter's pants, Logan breathed by my ear. "I'm going to make you feel so good, Maddie. We *all* are, and I can't wait to watch you come, again and again."

The promise in his words brought a gasp to my lips. While Dexter eased back to shed his pants, Logan pulled my shirt up over my head. Then his hands were cupping my breasts, his thumbs swiveling over the peaks with enough force to send jolts of pleasure through my nipples even with the fabric of my bra in between us.

"Get her pants off too, Dex," Slade ordered in an unusually gruff voice.

As Beckett leaned in to steal another kiss for himself, the other guys peeled my jeans off me. A hand brushed over my panties. Then Slade chuckled. "There's a more fun way of removing those."

He must have motioned to Dexter, because two mouths pressed against my hips in unison. Their scorching breaths tingled over my thighs as they dragged my panties down by their teeth.

Then agile fingers delved right into the spot where I needed it most. I jerked into Dexter's eager hand, my eyes rolling back with the blissful sensation it conjured.

Logan groaned. "That's right, baby. We've got you."

Clothes were being shed all around me. The encounter was melding into a blur of passion and need. I could barely think, only move with the skillful touches stirring delight all through my body, arching to meet one kiss and then another.

Somewhere in there, my bra disappeared, baring my breasts to the warm air. Beckett's thumb and forefinger closed around one pert nipple. "Try this," he said to Logan, giving the slightest tug that drew a moan right out of my throat.

Logan smirked and repeated the gesture on the other side until I was writhing between the two of them, still bucking into Dexter's massaging fingers. My body shuddered, so close to release. Then my gaze caught on Slade, kneeling near me as he rubbed his hand over his stunningly erect shaft.

A different sort of desire reverberated through me. I parted my lips with a flick of my tongue.

"Come closer," I murmured. "I'm going to make you feel good too, Slade."

"Oh, Piccolina, you know I can't refuse an offer like that."

I flipped over onto my hands and knees between them and lowered my head to suck Slade's shaft into my mouth. His breath broke as I swirled my tongue around him, his hips pumping toward me instinctively.

His fingers tangled in my hair with the gentle tugs I loved.

Dexter had moved with me, continuing his attentions between my legs. He hooked a finger right inside me and exhaled shakily at my muffled moan.

"Do you want more than this inside you, Madelyn?" he asked in the sexiest voice I'd ever heard from him.

I hummed in what I hoped was a clear enough answer. There was a crinkling as a condom packet changed hands, and then Dexter adjusted my position so he could slide under me, gripping my hips as I straddled him.

His cock rubbed over my clit and then plunged right into me. I cried out around Slade's erection and then lapped it even more enthusiastically.

Slade jerked with my attentions, his fingers tightening in my hair. I sucked him down hard, and his breath hitched. He mumbled a curse as he spilled himself into my mouth. Then he lifted my head to kiss me with his taste still on my lips while I rocked over his friend.

When my mouth tore away from Slade's, Dexter reached around me to squeeze my ass. He curled his fingers right between my cheeks and grazed my other opening. Maybe it was something in my face, or maybe he'd seen signs from me before, but his lips curled with a pleased smile.

"I think she'd like to be filled here too," he said. "Who's going to take that honor?"

"That ass is mine," Logan growled, and I trembled with anticipation.

Dexter kept thrusting up into me, and Logan's hand replaced his friend's against my back entrance. With a rustling, someone must have passed him some lube, because a slick gel smoothed over my opening. He worked one finger and then another into me until I was moaning so loud I wondered if I was breaking Beckett's rule about not disturbing his father.

But the mafia heir didn't look concerned. He claimed my mouth, drinking in my desperate sounds as Logan slid his thick shaft into me from behind.

I'd never felt so stretched or so full... or so complete. I bowed over Dexter, shaking as my first orgasm blazed through me just like that.

All of my men were working together, encouraging each other as they gave me the time of my life. We really had gotten past all the animosity and jealousy. It was the five of us together, one cohesive team.

I wasn't going to neglect any part of that team myself. As I caught my breath, I reached down Beckett's well-muscled torso to his rigid erection. With a tight grip, I pumped my hand up and down.

"Fuck, that feels good, Maddie," he rasped, nipping my earlobe.

Logan and Dexter moved inside me in unison, pumping in and out with Dexter's hands on my waist and Logan's steadying my hips. Their rhythmic strokes pushed me right back to the brink again, the wave of pleasure expanding from my core.

I kept moving—kept pace as Logan roared and stiffened behind me. Dexter moved a hand between my thighs, the pressure on my clit sending my bliss spiraling even faster. He panted, holding on as long as he could, but he didn't need to wait much longer.

This time, the orgasm didn't rise and fall on the way to my peak. It came all at once, slamming into me like a tidal wave of ecstasy. It would have knocked me off my feet if I'd been standing.

Dexter let out a groan as he came with me. I slumped over him, my hand still clenched around Beckett's shaft, and had just enough wherewithal left to bend to the side and take the head of his cock into my mouth.

Beckett rocked between my lips hard and fast. I sucked him down as far as I could, and he came with a spurt of salty liquid and a strangled sound.

I collapsed between the four of them, and they sank down around me. I lay there perfectly surrounded, and for the first time since Beckett's call in the library what felt like a million years ago, a sense of peace settled over me.

That was what I felt surrounded by all of my men. A sense of everlasting peace and certainty. Unity and loyalty. Family.

The long, chaotic day finally caught up with me, and my eyelids drifted shut.

———

When I opened my eyes again, I barely remembered having fallen asleep. I definitely hadn't meant to. I blinked, staring at the four guys sprawled around me in the early morning sunlight drifting through the window.

Now that my exhaustion and shock had faded, the thought of how much they still didn't know hit me like a smack of cold water. I needed to tell them everything, lay it all out, as painful as some of it might be. We couldn't deal with the huge problem still facing us until we all understood what we were dealing with.

I stretched my legs. Slade jerked upright as my cool feet pressed into his side.

"Jesus," he muttered. "Keep those icicles to yourself."

His dark brown eyes met mine, glazed with sleep, but despite the complaint, his expression showed nothing but contentment.

"Could you shut the fuck up?" Logan groaned, rolling over and then rubbing his face.

Beckett chuckled, though his eyes hadn't yet opened. "Good morning to all of you too."

With a sigh in anticipation of the conversation ahead, I sat up.

Dexter peered up at me and pushed up on his elbows. "What's the matter?"

"There's a lot we still need to talk about," I said, measuring out my words. "A lot that I found out yesterday, about Doom's Seed and about Logan's mom."

I paused, studying Logan's reaction, but his mouth only tightened a little.

I forced myself to continue. "I think I know how they got involved, and what Doom's Seed is trying to cover up—as well as why he had my dad murdered."

CHAPTER
SIX

Madelyn

"...And then I shoved the dresser in front of the closet door and ran for it," I said, wrapping up my account of my kidnapping.

All four of my men were staring at me from their positions around the living room. Beckett and Logan had staked out the spots on either side of me on one of the sofas, and Slade and Dexter had each taken an armchair nearby.

For the first several seconds after I finished speaking, silence hung over the room. Logan's mouth had flattened into a tight line. Beckett's expression was stormy. Slade set his hands on his knees, balled into fists, and Dexter rubbed his hand across his frowning mouth.

"An illegal transplant service," he said, breaking the silence. "It does fit all the pieces. That must be what they were transporting in the poisonous fish coolers: the organs they got by some illegal means."

Beckett nodded grimly. "And the building we investigated yesterday will be where they performed at least some of the transplant operations in this area."

Slade shook his head in bemusement. "I guess people must be willing to pay a hell of a lot for a procedure that could make the difference between life and death."

The instant after he'd spoken, his gaze flicked to Logan. I hadn't spelled out the assumptions I'd made after hearing Yvonne's conversation with the man who must be Doom's Seed, but the implications were obvious.

Logan looked up at us. His voice came out strained and without his usual force. "And that has to be how my mom met Doom's Seed. She must have paid him to handle my liver transplant—there mustn't have been a match soon enough, and she got desperate."

"That would fit too," I said carefully, watching his expression. I had no idea how hard this must be for him. Not only had his mother totally abandoned him without him knowing, but it'd been to join a major criminal whose crimes she'd involved her nine-year-old son in too.

Logan bowed his head, and I reached over to grasp

his hand. He squeezed it back, taking a moment to gather himself again.

"It even makes sense why things were so tense between her and my dad after the operation," he said. "I don't think Dad has any idea how she pushed the operation forward, but she had to get that money from somewhere. At least one time I heard him saying something about their savings, and he mentioned more than once that he wasn't sure he could trust her anymore. She must have taken a bunch out and refused to tell him what for."

I stroked my thumb up and down the back of his hand, remembering the doubts he'd expressed in the past about whether he'd even deserved his second chance at life. How much more would this revelation have shaken his sense of self-worth?

"It was her choice, not yours," I reminded him. "You didn't get any say in it. And maybe she was wrong, and there would have been a liver by legitimate channels in time, and you getting the liver you did only meant that someone else's life got saved too."

Logan grimaced. "Still. The people he's getting those organs from must also be desperate—desperate or murdered. And now I…" He couldn't seem to finish, resting his hand on his abdomen over his scar instead.

Slade spoke up, equally tentative. "From what you said, it sounds like Yvonne's connection with Doom's Seed has gone beyond, er, professional? They're romantically involved?"

I tipped my head in reluctant acknowledgment, still

focused on Logan. "She was definitely talking to him as if they had a personal relationship, like they'd built a life together. He wasn't exactly affectionate, but he didn't dispute that idea either."

Dexter's hand skimmed upward to run through his rumpled black curls. "For her to fake her own death to run away with him, she would have needed pretty major motivation. Just feeling like she owed him for a service she paid for wouldn't cut it."

"No," Logan said with a ragged bark of a laugh that had no humor in it.

Beckett leaned forward, his hands clasped together on his lap. "Let's lay out what we know in the order it happened. Logan had his transplant operation—fourteen years ago?"

"Yeah."

"And I'm guessing your follow-up treatment was in the same hospital where Maddie's father worked, since that's the only one in your hometown."

"That's right," Logan said again, a little of his typical determined energy coming back into his voice. "That's how Evan could have stumbled on evidence. Maybe there was something in my post-op treatment that tipped him off that something wasn't quite right."

"That would make the most sense," I said. "If Doom's Seed has been running this scheme for a while, there've probably been other transplant patients of his at that hospital, but I wouldn't think there'd have been any others around the same time as you. It's not that big a town."

"So your dad started digging into Doom's Seed's dealings," Slade said slowly, "following whatever trail he'd gotten on, and once he got to the point of poking around those properties, Doom's Seed obviously caught on that something was up."

Dexter cocked his head. "If he was still in touch with Yvonne then, which seems likely, he'd have mentioned that this was someone from the same town she lived in. She'd have been worried that he was going to expose *her* as well as Doom's Seed."

Beckett raised his hands. "I don't think there's any need to pin the murder on her. Doom's Seed would have wanted to eliminate anyone trying to expose his illegal work without any extra factors in the mix."

"But she might have encouraged him to get on with it," Logan said, his jaw flexing. "She kidnapped Maddie at gunpoint. Brought her into a place where her lover could threaten to kill Maddie. She obviously doesn't have anywhere near as much of a conscience as I'd have wanted to believe."

"It doesn't really matter," I said. "Doom's Seed would have had his people set up the murder. But your mom hadn't left yet at that point."

"No. It was three years after my operation when she —when we *thought* she died." Logan sighed and sagged back against the sofa. "I guess she got sick of family life and found an escape so she could be with the psycho she'd fallen for permanently." His voice got hoarser. "Other people really *did* die in that explosion. She ran away from her responsibilities—and she was selfish enough to not care that she screwed up dozens of other lives in the process."

A gloomy silence descended over all of us. I had no idea how Yvonne justified any of her actions to herself. Maybe she blocked out everything from before she'd run away to join Doom's Seed, like that'd all been some other woman who didn't count anymore.

"That's everything," Slade said, sitting a little straighter. "We've got the whole story pieced together."

Dexter knit his brow. "Not exactly. We still can't *prove* any of this. Even the conversation Maddie overheard, if she gave testimony, a lot of what we've determined is making deductions rather than anything outright stated."

My heart leapt with a sudden jolt of hope. "I might have something that can help with that."

I scrambled off the sofa and found the purse I'd dropped beside it last night. Brandishing it like a trophy, I returned to the guys. "This is Yvonne's. I took it because she stuck my phone in it, but she'll have her own things inside. Things important enough that she wanted them within reach when she left home. There's got to be *something* useful in there."

Logan let out a chuckle that sounded less pained this time and pulled the purse out of my hands into his lap. "Maddie the purse thief. You never cease to amaze me. God, I love you."

My cheeks flushed even though he'd confessed those feelings before. It made me a bit giddy just seeing more of his enthusiasm for the investigation returning now that he had something concrete to delve into.

He dug through the purse and pulled out a phone that was definitely not mine.

Beckett whistled approvingly. "I'm guessing you can get a lot of mileage out of that."

Logan smiled at him. "And anything I can't crack, your tech people should be able to." A fiercer light came into his dark eyes as he considered the possibilities. "I'll go through the contacts and messages—and I need to check the records at all the hospitals in this city and the area around it for someone named Baldwin who had an organ transplant. If his file was the one your dad thought was the most important, it could be the key to blowing this whole thing wide open."

Slade rubbed his hands together. "I don't know how to hack, but I can definitely run searches on the records we already have."

Logan paused. His gaze dropped to his torso again. "We also have evidence in me. My liver is proof of what happened, no matter how well Mom and Doom's Seed covered their tracks. If we can connect it to the businesses Doom's Seed is running, then we can be sure he doesn't get away with any of this."

Beckett stood up, his tone calmly authoritative. "We'll cross that bridge when we come to it. In the meantime, let me know what you need so you can start hacking into those other hospital systems. I'll have my people help in whatever—"

The ring of his phone cut him off. Frowning,

Beckett dug it out of his pocket and raised it to his ear. "Beckett here."

A moment later, his stance went rigid, anger flaring in his normally cool gray eyes. "They *what?* Those pricks…" He sucked in a sharp breath. "Hang tight. I'll get you out of there—I just need to summon reinforcements."

My stomach had already knotted by the time he hung up and glanced around at us. "What's happening?" I asked, dreading the answer.

Beckett's fingers gripped the phone so hard his knuckles whitened. "He's not wasting any time showing his true intentions. Doom's Seed has launched another attack on my territory."

CHAPTER
SEVEN

Slade

Beckett paced the room, making one call and then another, delivering his orders in a taut but steady voice. Even when clearly upset, he carried himself with so much authoritative confidence that I couldn't help thinking I wanted to be him when I grew up, even though the guy was only a couple of years older than me.

As he finally lowered the phone to shove it into his pocket, he turned toward us.

"What's happening?" Maddie asked quickly, her pale face tight with concern. "Are your people okay?"

Of course that would be her first thought—the human lives on the line. A pang of affection ran through my chest alongside my jangling nerves.

Beckett shook his head. "Not all of them, and none of them might be if I don't get out there quick. My family has a farm not far from here that we use for stashing goods when we need a temporary holding spot. Doom's Seed must have figured that out, and his people are trying to ransack the place."

Shit. "And some of your men were there?" I said.

"Yeah. A bunch of them were on the property handling a new shipment. Two are already down. The rest managed to get inside one of the buildings and barricade the entrance, but now they're stuck. It's a fucking siege. And even if we only lose the items in those buildings, they're valuable—it'll shatter the trust of the clients who were counting on getting their purchases."

He shoved a hand back through his blond hair, rumpling the normally sleek strands, and turned toward the door. "I've called as many reinforcements as I can to take on the attackers, but the men here at the house can get out there fastest—and I need to go with them. Keep their spirits up, show that we're in this together. I can't let my people face this kind of shit alone."

Those words only solidified the respect I'd come to feel for this guy, regardless of his criminal associations. Beckett was good at what he did—and he clearly tried to handle things in much better ways than assholes like this Doom's Seed prick. I didn't like the idea of him getting screwed over—especially when it was happening partly because he'd tried to help us out.

I sprang to my feet with a surge of conviction. "We'll help too—we'll do whatever we can."

I'd already known Logan and Dexter would agree with me on that. They both stood too, their expressions determined.

"Absolutely," Logan said.

"And even though you probably didn't mean me," Maddie said, getting up with a swish of her pale hair over her shoulders, "you aren't leaving me behind. There's got to be some way I can pitch in."

Beckett glanced back at us, a darker shadow crossing his face. "This could get pretty bad. They're actively shooting at anyone they can, and we'll be the first ones on the scene."

Logan flexed his shoulders. "Then let's go show them that they can't mess with you without consequences. You didn't turn your back on us even when we were being jerks to you, so we're sure as hell not leaving you in the lurch."

Maddie nodded. "We're in this together," she said quietly. "All of this is our fight too. I want to see Doom's Seed taken down as much as anyone."

More, no doubt, given what we'd figured out about her dad's death. I shot her a tight but supportive smile.

Beckett searched our expressions as if looking for any sign of uncertainty. He didn't want to waste time on arguments, I could tell.

"All right," he said, marching toward the door. "Come on. We'll get equipped in the van. I already have the men downstairs prepping it."

We hustled down the stairs and out a back door, where we found a van larger than the one we'd taken before idling. One of Beckett's employees saluted him from the driver's seat, another poised next to him.

"This bunch is coming too?" the driver asked with obvious confusion.

"They're with me," Beckett said. "They're pretty handy in a fight. Let's get out there and defend what's ours."

We leapt into the back of the van where two more guys were crouched with a large canvas duffle bag at their feet. They must have heard Beckett's exchange with the driver, because they didn't question our arrival. One of them jerked open the zipper on the bag and put the contents on display.

"Grab whatever you want first, boss. We've got lots of extra ammo too."

"Perfect." Beckett motioned us over. "Pick out whatever weapons you'll be most comfortable with. We should all go in armed."

Logan pulled his pistol out from his pocket. "I think I'll stick with the firearm I'm already familiar with."

"Fair enough." Beckett turned to Dexter, who'd come up beside him, swaying with the swerving of the van down the driveway. "How about you?"

Dexter knelt down to catch his balance and studied the array of weaponry with typical precision. He pulled out a pair of long, deadly-looking knives and tested them in his hands.

I saw him hesitate and suspected he was thinking of

the attacker years ago he'd needed to stab to save my life. But he didn't shy away from the blades. He eased away from the bags and set them on the floor of the van beside him.

I went over next with a twist of dread in my gut. Fighting wasn't really my thing. *Killing* wasn't my thing at all, even if I'd had to do it once. I wanted to beat these bastards down, but if I could manage that without slaughtering them left and right, it'd rest easier on my conscience.

My gaze fell on a steel shaft buried amid the guns and knives. I carefully dug out the baton, extended it to its full length, and swung it through the air. A little of the tension inside me released.

It was solid and heavy enough to crack a bone, but not the sort of automatic death a shot or a stab would ensure. It kind of reminded me of the bars built into my prosthetic leg. In a way, I was extending the reach of my arm with this weapon just like the prosthetic extended my malformed leg so I could get things done more easily.

Something about that thought felt right. I sank down next to Dexter with a sense of satisfaction that I hadn't been able to summon before.

Beckett had pulled a couple of guns and a knife from the bags, arming himself more thoroughly than the rest of us. When he looked at Maddie, she grimaced.

"My training is mostly in hand-to-hand combat—assuming I won't have a weapon or at best I'll have to make use of whatever random thing I can get hold of. I'd be afraid I'd shoot one of the people on our side if I tried to use a gun."

He handed her a switchblade, the knife edge folded in. "At least keep this in your pocket, just in case." Glancing back at the duffel bag, he hummed to himself. "I think we might be able to set this up so that you don't need to do much fighting at all."

Maddie bristled automatically. "I *can* fight."

Beckett held up his hands. "I know, believe me. But out of the five of us, I'm guessing that you have the least experience tangling with people who are more than happy to kill you if they get the chance."

Maddie hesitated and then sighed in resignation. "Okay, that's a fair assessment."

"You'll still play a crucial role," he assured her. "We'll just keep you out of the worst part of the fray as much as possible." He patted the bag beside him before zipping it up. "My men under siege need to replenish their weapons and ammo, and you can be the one to deliver the goods. The rest of us will cover you."

A smile crossed my lips despite myself. Not only was Beckett determined to keep Maddie as safe as possible, he'd figured out an argument even she had to accept. Something Logan had failed at more times than I could count.

Beckett got on his phone again, checking how close his reinforcements were and then how things were going on the farm. After the last call, his mouth had tightened.

"We're almost there," he said. "And we're going to go straight in. Do exactly what I say, and I think we can all come out of this all right."

The van tore down the road and around another corner. Beckett moved to the door, bracing himself by the handle with one pistol already at the ready. He tipped his head to us, a signal to prepare ourselves to spring into action.

"We're going to barrel right through the middle of the Doom's Seed contingent, as close to the barn door as we can get. Someone's waiting at the door to let Maddie in the second she reaches it. Maddie, you jump out and run straight to the door—it'll be around the right side of the van. My men in the front of the van will hold off anyone who comes at us from that side, and the rest of us will defend the rear. We'll use the van for cover with the barn at our backs. Got it?"

We all nodded. A metallic clinking carried from the front of the van—the sound of a rifle being cocked, I realized. My stomach flipped over.

Maddie was slinging the straps of the duffel bag over her shoulder. She hefted it to make sure she could carry its weight and then set it down again. I couldn't stop myself from pushing off the floor to go join her.

I touched her cheek. "Never a dull day around here, huh, Piccolina?"

She laughed roughly. "I'm looking forward to some boredom when all this is over."

"Oh, I'm sure we'll find ways to spice up everyday life—ways much more enjoyable than this." I tipped her face to meet mine and claimed a quick but emphatic kiss that I hoped told her how far I intended to go to guarantee we got that future.

I stepped back, grasping my baton. The driver gave a brisk shout. Then the van screeched to a halt, and we all sprang into motion.

Beckett whipped open the back doors and used them as a shield, taking a few shots out the back and then around the side. At the swivel of his arm, the rest of us charged forward.

Logan leapt out first and fired a shot of his own. More booms rang out from the front of the van, along with the thuds of bullets drilling into the van's wall. A fine sweat broke out over my skin, but I sprang out alongside Maddie without letting my fear hold me back.

Maddie dashed around the side of the van with the duffel bags in tow. I shoved between her and a burly tattooed guy who lunged at her and smacked him across the side of the head with my baton.

He reeled to the side and yanked out a gun, but before he could take aim, I slammed the baton even harder into his wrist. At the crunch of breaking bone and a pained grunt, the pistol dropped from his hand.

Dexter was slicing out at another attacker who'd gotten close to the back of the van. Logan and Beckett were still firing, but the swarm of Doom's Seed people was all around us. I lashed out at another who charged in close and pushed farther out of our temporary shelter to crack the forearm of a prick with a revolver.

The bang of the closing door sounded behind me,

making my nerves jump for a second before its meaning sank in.

Maddie had gotten inside the barn. Maddie was safe—well, as safe as she could be while these assholes still had the whole area under siege.

We had to make sure they didn't make it to the door to follow her.

I threw myself even more into the battle, the pound of my heart egging me on more than unnerving me now. Every swing of the baton and every body I struck down was one more act to keep Maddie safe and fend off the pricks who thought they could hurt all of us.

My leg didn't once wobble beneath me. I whacked and bashed alongside the other guys with rhythmic rasps of breath until more cars and vans roared into view beyond the fray.

Beckett's reinforcements had arrived.

A grin sprang to my face, and I shoved away a man who'd hurtled toward me. Spinning around, I clocked him right across the forehead. My grip tightened around my baton, exhilaration and renewed strength surging through my body.

It didn't matter that my limbs weren't quite as whole as the other guys' or that my prosthetic put me at a potential disadvantage. I was giving the fight my all and holding my own.

We weren't going to let the real bad guys win. Not today.

CHAPTER
EIGHT

Madelyn

Staring at the bodies sprawled across the terrain around the barn, I couldn't help trying to tell myself that they weren't dead. They were just unconscious. Knocked out or fainted from their injuries, but there was still a chance…

The attempt wasn't convincing even to myself. Blood splattered most of those bodies. A few within my view were gazing at nothing with eyes that never blinked.

Death was all around. I only hoped that most of them were Doom's Seed's people and not Beckett's.

"It's… it's a mess," Logan said roughly from where he was standing beside me.

I hugged myself. "At least the four of you made it

through okay. And I'll try to make sure that as many other people do as I possibly can as well."

Beckett hustled over with a plastic first aid box brought in one of the cars of reinforcements. "Here," he said. "I can show you who we need to patch up. The doctor we have on staff is on his way, but you're the only person on site right now with significant medical experience."

I nodded stiffly and pushed myself into motion. I knew I wasn't a doctor or even a nurse, but I *had* been training for this kind of work for years. If I could save even one life or at least a limb, what better time to start putting my studies into real practice?

As Beckett motioned for me to follow him, two of his men walked past us, hauling one of those blankly staring corpses. They tossed it into the back of a van. My stomach lurched.

I tried to focus on Beckett, but my gaze veered to a man slumped on the ground whose entire skull had been blasted open down to his bearded jaw. A horrified squeak escaped me.

Then Beckett was there, gripping my chin to pull my gaze to him. I met his solemn gray eyes, my pulse rattling through my veins.

"This is how my line of work goes sometimes," he said. "Not very often, thankfully. And I never like it when it does. But I swear to you, we only kill when it's that or be killed ourselves. I'd rather you'd stayed back at the house and not had to see all this."

I squared my shoulders, willing down my nausea.

"No, it's okay. I asked to be here—I wanted to help, and I still do." And I could do something no one else here right now could.

Beckett pressed a quick kiss to my forehead and led me the rest of the way to a man who was leaning against the tire of a pickup truck. He was clutching his arm in front of him, blood still seeping from wounds in his shoulder and forearm. I had the impression someone had sliced him open with a knife.

"He'll probably need stitches," I said, crouching next to him on the trampled grass. "And to have the wounds properly cleaned first. I don't think I can do a good enough job with this." I waved the kit.

"The doctor can handle the most serious parts," Beckett said. "Can you stop the bleeding for the time being?"

I pulled out a roll of gauze and a couple of thicker pads from the kit. "I think so." I focused on the man in front of me. "Can you lift up your arm a little so I can wrap it?"

The guy hesitated and then glanced up at Beckett. Beckett offered him a gentle smile. "She knows what she's doing. She's studying to be a doctor herself."

At his reassurance, the man visibly relaxed. What Beckett said meant that much to him—he trusted his boss without question.

That was the kind of man I'd fallen for: the kind who ruled through respect rather than fear. Who cared about everyone working under him rather than seeing them as game pieces on a board.

He was a good leader, and he didn't deserve to be in this situation. In this war that was brewing in a large part because of the way the Vigil guys and I had enraged Doom's Seed by investigating my dad's murder.

Grimacing at that thought, I swabbed the man's arm and shoulder with rubbing alcohol, apologizing when he hissed at the sting, and wrapped both wounds as tightly as I could. When no blood made it through to the outer layer of gauze, I let out my breath in relief.

"I think that should keep you stable well enough until the actual doctor gets here," I told him. "I'm sorry I couldn't do more."

His smile was tight, but I could see the gratitude in it. "Thank you for trying."

Beckett guided me on to another man who was bleeding from a wide but shallow gash on his head where he'd been clipped by a bullet, and then to a woman who I was pretty sure had fractured her ankle and who cursed a blue streak when I eased it into a makeshift splint to stabilize it.

I had no idea what the gang's foot soldiers made of me at first glance, this preppy college-aged girl carrying a basic first aid kit, but as soon as Beckett spoke of my expertise, they offered themselves up for treatment without hesitation. The next man I checked out, who had a stab wound in his thigh, even told me I should go ahead and stitch him up myself.

"I really think it's better if you wait for the doctor," I told him. "If I miss something and you get an infection, that could be just as deadly as the bleeding."

Beckett checked his phone. "He's just fifteen minutes away now. We'll get you good as new."

The man grinned shakily. "I know you will, boss."

After doing what I could for another man who'd taken a bullet to the calf, Beckett waved me over to the van we'd arrived in. "That's everyone who needs looking after. I've got a bunch of other things to take care of. You can take a breather in the back if you want to get away from all this at least a little."

As he hurried off, I glanced around, noting Logan and Slade helping haul another corpse into the other van. A brisk breeze blew over me, and the back of my arm stung.

Frowning, I twisted my arm at the shoulder and craned my neck, reaching toward the spot with my opposite hand at the same time. My fingers touched damp, severed fabric, provoking another jab of pain.

Sometime during the fight, I'd gotten a cut on the back of my arm. It was shallow—it looked like it'd only just bleed all the way through my torn shirt sleeve. The adrenaline must have numbed me to the pain before now.

I still had the first aid kit, now tucked under my arm, but it'd be hard to bandage up that spot when I could barely even get a look at it.

"What happened?" someone asked sharply from behind me.

I turned, recognizing the voice but not quite believing it until I saw Dexter taking the last couple of strides to reach me. His black curls were even messier than usual, his pale face tight with strain, but his green eyes caught mine with all the intensity he usually brought to bear.

"I'm okay," I reassured him, my pulse fluttering at the concern etched in his expression. "But I could use a little help patching myself up… if you don't mind."

I held my hand partway toward him, letting him decide how far to take the physical contact. Dexter gripped my fingers without hesitation and carefully rotated my arm to the side so he could examine the wound.

He sucked in a breath through clenched teeth with a hiss. "We were supposed to get you to the building without you getting hurt."

"It can't be that bad if I only just noticed it. There were a lot of people fighting—I'm lucky this is all that happened."

The frown didn't leave his face. "*You* weren't even fighting." His gaze darted up to briefly meet mine again. "Tell me what I need to do to bandage it properly."

I had no doubt he'd follow my every instruction to the letter. I wiggled the first aid kit out from under my other arm and moved to the back of the van where I could set it down. Once I'd popped it open, I handed him the bottle of rubbing alcohol and a patch of gauze. "We should roll up the sleeve to completely uncover it, and then you can swab it with the alcohol. That'll disinfect it."

He nodded and helped me tug the ragged sleeve of the T-shirt up to my shoulder. Then he splashed rubbing alcohol on the gauze. I braced myself as he raised it to my arm. He swiped it over the entire area swiftly but thoroughly while I gritted my teeth against the burning sensation.

Dexter's attention flicked to my face, and he jerked his hand back. "I'm hurting you."

I offered him a tight but genuine smile. "That's actually a good thing. It means all the things I *wouldn't* want lingering in the wound are dying. But I think it's clean enough now."

With a grim expression, he set down the pad. "Now what?"

I peered at the wound as well as I could. It was definitely shallow, like someone had raked a knife across my arm without managing to really dig it in. Only a few beads of blood were welling up along the cleaned skin.

"More gauze," I said. "That should be enough to stop the bleeding completely and keep it clean for the time being. Cut off a strip a couple of feet long and wrap it around my arm. I'll tell you how much pressure is good. And there's tape to fix the end once you're done."

He got to work with the same brisk efficiency he brought to almost every task, but his fingers brushed against my skin with so much gentleness that my heart swelled with affection. I couldn't imagine what it'd been like for him racing into this battle when he was most comfortable snapping photos and piecing together data.

But he'd done it for Beckett—and for me.

"Thank you," I said when he'd taped the bandage in place.

Dexter eased my sleeve down and stared at the bloody edges of fabric for a moment. His eyes hardened in a way I'd never seen from him before.

"Do you know who it was who cut you?" he asked abruptly.

I shook my head, puzzled. "Like I said, I didn't even notice it'd happened until just now."

Dexter's voice roughened. "I wish I knew. If I find out, I'll do so much worse to them."

The vehemence in his voice, full of so much dark promise, sent a shiver over my skin. It wasn't entirely unappealing, but it startled me.

"That doesn't sound like you," I couldn't help saying.

Dexter lifted his head. This time he let his gaze linger on mine, even though I suspected the eye contact wasn't entirely comfortable for him.

"I can't help feeling that way," he said. "Like I'd tear apart anyone who even tries to hurt you. I—I *love* you, and the idea of losing you… I'd rather face a million unsolvable puzzles than ever face that possibility again."

A lump rose in my throat. I turned to him and pulled him into a hug, squeezing him hard. He returned the embrace as if he never planned to let go of me. His warmth wrapped around me, making the emotion that'd already filled my chest expand through my whole body.

"I love you too," I said, hoping he could hear how much I meant that. "And I plan on staying right here with you no matter what those assholes try to do."

I just hoped we could figure out the puzzle we were in the middle of before anyone else got hurt.

Madelyn

You wouldn't think watching a guy type on a laptop keyboard could be all that thrilling, but something about the intensity in Logan's expression and the urgency with which his fingers flew over the keys sent a tingle through me as I watched.

Of course, it didn't hurt that I also considered him to be one of the most gorgeous men on the planet.

My other favorite men were gathered around me in Beckett's usual white van: Beckett in the driver's seat up front, Slade sitting on one of the benches in the back next to me with a reassuring hand on my thigh, and Dexter perched on the opposite bench beside Logan, his eyes glued to a tablet.

Voices carried through the wall of the van from

outside. We'd parked near one of the city's hospitals, as close as we dared to the building. The emergency ward wasn't far away, and cars and taxis were constantly roaring by, dropping off people who hustled or limped through the doors.

At the wail of an ambulance, I tensed. But just as the siren cut out, Logan's head jerked up. "I've got it! All the records they have digitized. We can get out of here."

He'd hacked into the hospital's database with the help of a few tips from Beckett's tech crew, meaning to download every file he could get his hands on. This was our second stop so far, but we weren't finished yet.

Beckett glanced back at me. "Where do you think we should go next, soon-to-be-Dr. Silver?"

I couldn't help smiling at the title despite the tension filling the van. "There's St. Joseph's out in the suburbs. That's the next closest hospital."

He nodded and put the van into drive.

As it pulled away from the curb, Logan kept tapping away at his computer. "I'm transferring a bunch more transplant patient files over to you," he told Dexter. "I think I was able to separate out most of them right away, but I'm going to do a more thorough scan to make sure I didn't miss anything."

Dexter nodded without looking up from the tablet. He'd been studying the records Logan had dug up, piecing together potential patterns that might indicate which ones had been falsified to cover up an illegal transplant.

He clicked his tongue against his teeth. "Here's

another one. This is the fifth file I've found with a red blood cell count of 4.47 million per microliter. Other than that, I haven't seen the exact same number in any of the records."

I frowned. "So they could be using data from previous legit records, an example of what they know things should look like to make their fake ones look correct."

He nodded. "There are a couple of other markers, like kidney function, where I'm seeing some repetition, although not all in the same files. They were being cautious, using a few different examples to mix and match, I think. But once you start noticing the pattern, it's obvious."

Slade stretched out his prosthetic leg with a soft thump on the thinly carpeted floor. "And you said they all make it look like the actual transplant happened at some other hospital, right?"

Dexter nodded. "All the files I've collected with at least one repeated number were transfer patients. It makes sense—they wouldn't want to pretend the transplant happened at the same hospital where they received after care, which the staff could easily realize wasn't true."

Excitement jittered through my chest. We were getting so close, catching the key details of evidence that could expose Doom's Seed's illegal operations.

"It makes sense that the staff wouldn't have noticed the discrepancy like this," I said. "How many years were those patients spread across?"

"The oldest one I've found was from twenty-six years ago," Dexter said. "And I've set aside twelve records so far."

"So that's less than one case a year. Between that and the mixing and matching, and how many patients the doctors and nurses would typically be seeing, it's no wonder no one else noticed the repeated data. We never would have if we didn't know to look for it."

Beckett spoke up from behind the wheel. "Doom's Seed must have some kind of shell company set up to transfer the records over in a way that looks legit."

I nodded. "That could be another lead, if we can figure out where they're coming from."

Slade glanced toward Beckett. "How far do you think this business extends? Obviously it's not just this city since it covers our hometown as well. Presumably he's active in the entire region in between too."

"Given the reach of the average Devil's Dozen member," Beckett said, "I'd expect he's organizing the transplants throughout the state, at the very least. It's more likely he has connections and facilities set up in various places across the country. It could extend overseas as well."

The immensity of the crime momentarily overwhelmed me. My stomach lurched, and I wrapped my arms around myself. "We have to stop him."

Slade squeezed my shoulder. "We will. No doubt about it."

Logan jerked straighter upright in his seat, sucking in a breath. "Holy shit."

All our gazes except Beckett's shot to him.

"What?" I demanded.

He lifted his head to stare at us with a stunned expression. "I found it. The Baldwin file. It's *here*, in the latest batch of records. This has got to be it."

I sprang across the van to squeeze next to him on the bench and peer at his screen. Slade hustled over as well, leaning to peek over the top, and Dexter set aside his tablet to give the momentous occasion his full attention.

Logan motioned to the top of the record he had open on his laptop. The patient's name was Christina Baldwin.

"She had a dual kidney transplant," he said. "Sixteen years ago—not too long before Maddie's dad was killed."

"Remind me what's important about this particular file?" Beckett said.

While I started scanning the record, Slade filled the other guy in. "Logan found a bunch of old notes that Evan Silver wrote. Notes that seemed to be related to his investigation. A few of them mentioned the Baldwin file in a way that made it sound like it was some kind of key to his findings. We never knew what was in it or why he fixated on it, though."

"This could be the thing that tipped him off that something was wrong," I said, still skimming over the data as quickly as I could while still absorbing it. "The file passed by him for one reason or another while he was doing his usual research work... Wait a second. Scroll back up to the basic physical data?"

Logan complied, watching me instead of the screen. "What did you notice?"

I checked the woman's height and weight and confirmed what I'd thought I remembered. "She was really petite. Only four-foot-ten, ninety pounds."

Dexter cocked his head. "What made you want to check that?"

"Because down here..." I motioned for Logan to scroll back down, and he did until I tapped the screen. "The dosage of medication it says she was given to slow her heart rate for the transplant procedure. I did a project that touched on that drug earlier this year. That's definitely too high a dose for a person that small. It could have *stopped* her heart."

Logan's eyebrows rose. "But obviously it didn't, since she has a bunch more post-transplant records."

"It's probably not what they gave her at all—I'd bet it's another one of those copied numbers, and whoever put together this falsified document wasn't quite careful enough."

"Let me see." Dexter peered closer and then started tapping on his tablet. He let out a triumphant sound. "There are three more records just in the ones I already have with the exact same dosage. That's another marker —I hadn't caught that one yet."

Slade smiled tightly down at me. "Something like that—you figure your dad might have noticed the error."

"Absolutely. If it stood out to me, it'd have been even more obvious to him." I sucked my lower lip under my teeth to worry at it.

"Wow," Dexter said abruptly. "I found a record with that dosage from all the way back in the 1980s. How old was Doom's Seed then?"

"It could be part of his family legacy, a business that his parents were running before him," Beckett reminded us. "A lot of the ventures *I'm* involved with go back as far as my grandparents or even earlier."

The size of this psychopath's horrific practices and their impact on my world just kept expanding. I rubbed my forehead, my thoughts spinning as I tried to absorb it all.

"And they've gotten away with it for all this time," Logan muttered. "For fuck's sake."

Beckett's voice lowered. "You don't get this high up in the criminal world without being very good at covering your tracks. We're incredibly lucky to even come across that one obvious slip in forty or more years of records."

It all made sense, in the most sickening sort of way. I gazed out the van window with a growing sense of melancholy, watching the buildings whip by.

Beckett turned the vehicle into another parking lot outside a big brick building. "Here's St. Joseph's." He turned in his seat to check with Logan. "Are you good to get started?"

Logan flexed his fingers. "I'm ready. Let's see what we can dig up here."

As he resumed his urgent typing, Slade grabbed my hand and tugged me back to the other bench. "He's not great company while he's at work, Piccolina," he said with a wink. "And you've already figured out the key the rest of us couldn't."

I didn't feel all that victorious, though. My stomach churned as Logan dug into the hospital's network and siphoned out copies of their files.

"Transplants, transplants," he muttered to himself, and then to Dexter, "Sending more over." He wasn't even waiting to finish the download before passing some on now.

Dexter's fingers flicked across his tablet's screen. "Here's one. Two of the figures I've seen repeated." He paused, his eyes darting from side to side as he scanned the screen. "Another—this one has the same dosage of that medication as the Baldwin file."

I slumped back against the wall of the van. The participants in the awful scheme were everywhere. How many lives had Doom's Seed ruined or outright ended to get all those organs?

"How can we prove what's going on, even with these records?" I asked. "There's nothing clear enough in the files to get the cops to take notice, is there? They'd brush it off as coincidences or data error."

Slade's jaw clenched. "Then we find people with medical knowledge who'll understand it the same way you and your dad did."

"But I already had all this other evidence to convince me there was a problem, and my dad pieced it together on his own. Any doctor or researcher we try to tell is going to dismiss us as crazy before we even get far enough for them to pay attention to the data."

"Once we have enough pieces, they'll have to listen," Logan insisted, but I could tell from the grimness of his expression that he didn't totally believe that either.

We had a whole lot of records that claimed those operations had happened legitimately and only the smallest of signs that it was a lie. Doom's Seed obviously had actual doctors under his sway, because someone had performed those operations. I could already imagine that if we tracked down the facilities where the records said the transplants had taken place, he'd have all the proof in place to make it look legit, and the only people who'd know it wasn't true on his payroll.

We still needed something concrete and unarguable to tie our case together, and I had no idea where we were going to find that.

Logan

"Hey," Beckett called from across the room. "I figured I'd grab takeout for dinner. Does Mexican sound okay to you?"

I glanced up from the screen I'd been peering at, taking a second to reorient myself to the room around me—the opulent sitting room of what Beckett called his "apartment" in his family's mansion. It was safe to say I'd never lived anyplace that looked remotely like this. I'd never even had a vacation this fancy.

Not that our stay here was any kind of leisure situation.

"Sure," I said. "I think we all like that."

"I'll get a bunch of different things so there's lots of variety and people can choose what they like. If Slade and Dexter come back before I do, let them know I won't be long." He tipped his head to me and headed out.

My friends had gone out to take a stroll around the grounds after Slade had suggested they needed fresh air and exercise to clear their heads. Maddie had vanished into her guest bedroom to catch up on schoolwork—as well as she could with everything that was going on.

But I'd had a different kind of work to occupy me, one I'd been able to tell couldn't wait any longer after what we'd seen at the hospitals.

I picked up Mom's phone again, the one we'd found in the purse Maddie had stolen, and flicked to the next number in her Contacts list. When I ran a search on it on my laptop, it brought up the same name as it showed in her Contacts list: Celena's Nail Salon.

The website for the salon looked legit. I dug a little farther to see if I could find any connections to Doom's Seed's holdings, but it appeared the woman who owned the business was leasing the space from a perfectly above-board retail rental company.

Mom simply went there to get her nails done, presumably.

I sighed and slumped deeper into the leather couch cushions. That was basically all I'd turned up so far: Mom's personal service people. She had a hairdresser and a personal shopper and a stylist within easy dialing, and various shops and eateries. It was almost as if she had no social life at all, at least not with anyone she didn't pay.

Well, no social life outside Doom's Seed himself. I'd found a text thread going back years with an unlisted number that had to be him, given the explicit nature of some of the conversations it contained. Just remembering some of their exchanges made my stomach lurch.

Not only had my mother run off on me and Dad, but she'd done it so she could go around fucking a criminal scumbag every which way.

More and more, I found I couldn't even really think of her as my mom now. My real mom had died eleven years ago.

This woman—this monster who fawned over murderous crime lords and kidnapped innocent people—wasn't any part of my family.

Somehow she'd managed to keep anything business-related, at least when it came to her new lover's business, out of her phone. None of the service providers and shops I'd looked up had any connection to him even with extra digging to confirm. And when I'd scrolled back through their direct conversations, skimming the worst bits with a wince, I hadn't come across anything but the vaguest mentions of his illicit activities.

Comments like, "I've got a few things to deal with before I make it back to the apartment" weren't going to justify a warrant, let alone convict the prick for his crimes.

Even though I'd tried it already, I ran his number through my various tracking methods. All of them made it clear that the digits belonged to a burner phone with no specific information tied to it other than the basic provider.

If he called Mom's phone, I'd have had the chance to trace his immediate location with the right equipment, but otherwise the information was useless. And the chances of him calling when Mom would have told him about the stolen purse by now were pretty much nil.

I scrolled farther back through her message history, searching for any numbers not in her Contacts. I'd gone back to almost a year ago when the ringtone pealed out, sudden and loud enough that I nearly dropped the phone.

Closing my fingers around it, I stared at the screen. *Unknown caller*, the notification said. The ringtone sounded again.

My heart was thudding. I had no idea who this was —but shouldn't I make use of the best piece of evidence we'd gotten in every possible way? Maybe the caller would give away something we could work with.

Not that anyone could possibly mistake my voice for my mom's. But what the hell.

Just as the third ring sounded, I hit the answer button and brought the phone to my ear. "Hello?"

On the other end, the caller sucked in a startled breath. Then a far-too-familiar voice slipped from the speaker into my ear. "Hello, Logan."

It was Mom, calling her own phone. Probably trying to find out what had happened to it. Her greeting sounded as hesitant as I felt, not the coolly confident persona she'd put on when she'd spoken to me outside the medical facility.

Maybe that should have reassured me. I should have played it cool and calm like she had before. But at the sound of my name from her deceitful mouth, a surge of rage flared inside me. I couldn't contain myself.

"What the hell, Mom?" I burst out.

The question encompassed so much of my anger and hurt—that she'd left, that she'd let us believe she was dead, that she'd made me party to a crime without me even realizing it. That she'd kidnapped the woman I loved and brought her to where the vilest man in existence might have killed her.

None if it made sense. All of it made me want to scream into the phone, but I managed to contain *that* impulse.

"I'm sorry, sweetheart," she said, in exactly the voice I remembered from when I'd been a kid. "I didn't want any of this to happen this way."

"What do you mean?" I demanded. "None of it happened by accident. You didn't just stumble and end up running off with a criminal overlord or faking your own death."

Her tone hardened a little in response to mine. "There's a lot you don't know or understand. How could you? You were only a child."

A scoffing sound burst out of me. "Yeah, exactly. I was a child—I was your *son*—and you left me. You let me believe that you'd died. So you could live it up with some rich asshole?"

"He's a lot more than that," Mom said sternly. "You have no idea what you're talking about. I did what I needed to for my own sanity."

Was she even hearing herself? She thought abandoning her normal family to hook up with a psychotic crime boss was the *sane* option?

"If you were that unhappy, you could have just asked for a divorce," I retorted. "Then at least I'd still have been able to see you. I wouldn't have mourned you and gone to visit a grave that didn't really mean anything."

"It wasn't that simple."

I knew that, actually. My stomach churned before I forced out the words. "Right. Because as long as you were with me and known to be alive, you could be prosecuted for your crime. You didn't get the liver for my transplant by any method the police would approve of, did you, Mom?"

Even as the question spilled bitterly from my lips, some tiny part of me held on to a shred of hope that she'd tell me I was wrong about that one thing, that her shitty decisions hadn't tainted even me.

Her resigned sigh snuffed out that hope in an instant.

"I'm not going to apologize for *that*," she said stiffly. "I did what I needed to do to keep you alive. That's what a mother *should* do."

"You couldn't have just waited and let me get a new liver the regular way?"

"No. It was becoming so clear that there wouldn't be

a match from a legitimate source in time. Your other organs were starting to fail. I took the one option I came across that would save your life, and I don't regret that for a second."

I closed my eyes, willing down my nausea. I'd already known it had to be true, but hearing her admit to the crime sickened me all over again, even more than when the revelation had first hit me.

"You did all that, supposedly for me," I said. "And then you chucked me aside like I was nothing."

"Logan, I wasn't happy. I loved you more than anything, but with your father holding me back, I was trapped. I couldn't have continued being a good mother to you while I was stuck like that—I could already tell I was failing you. What I did—what I had to do—was the only way I could get out."

"Get out? You had a kid and a husband. A good mother shouldn't even *want* to get out of that situation. You should want to be with your family."

"I put you and Holand first for years, and I lost myself to it. I leapt at the first chance I'd had at real happiness in over a decade. I gave you as many years as I could, and then I made a clean break so you could get over it quickly."

Did she really think that was how it worked? Hadn't she ever missed *me*?

I couldn't bring myself to ask that question.

"*This* man makes you so happy?" I said instead. "He kills people—he had Maddie's father murdered! He doesn't care at all about who he destroys if they're in his way. How could a monster like that make you happy?"

"There's so much more to him than that," Mom insisted.

I shook my head. No, I'd given myself the answer already. The problem was that my mother was plenty monstrous too. I just hadn't realized it before.

She'd had moments in this conversation when she'd sounded a little sad. The slightest bit regretful. Was there any part of her that *wasn't* a monster?

There had to be, didn't there? How else could she have convinced me so well that she cared about me back when she'd been in my life for all those years?

"Mom," I said, my voice getting rough, "we could end this here. No matter how much more there is to him, he's causing dozens, probably hundreds of deaths. You can stop him. Turn him in to the police. Save all the people he's going to kill before it happens."

"Sweetheart, you know I can't do that."

"No, I don't know that! You're a witness— you know all kinds of things, I'm sure. You could say what happened with me and Maddie's dad. It's the only way you could make up for all the other things you've screwed up."

Mom's voice stiffened again. "I may have made mistakes, but I did the best with the options I had. I love this man. I'm happy with the life I've made for myself. You have no idea what I've been through or what the bigger picture looks like."

There was a click, and the line went dead. It took me a few seconds to process that she'd hung up on me.

I lowered the phone and set it down on the coffee table. My shoulders slumped, my entire body seeming to have been drained of energy.

I could tell myself that she wasn't really my mother over and over, but that didn't stop the knowledge of who she was from lacing through me like a knife to the gut.

The door to the sitting room swung open. I sat up straighter, expecting to see Beckett or my friends, but it was Maddie who poked her head in.

"Hey," she said softly. "I heard you talking when I came up on the door... You sounded pretty upset. Is everything okay?"

I swallowed thickly and pressed my hand to my forehead. "Yes. And no. It was—I was going through my mom's phone, and she called it, I guess to see where it'd ended up. And we talked. It wasn't a pleasant conversation."

Maddie grimaced and slipped inside. She hustled straight to the sofa and sat down beside me, wrapping her arm around my back.

"I can only imagine. Did she say anything that would help us with the case?"

I shook my head. "I even tried to convince her to help directly by turning on Doom's Seed, but she wouldn't consider it. She says she *loves* him." Acid filled my tone.

Maddie winced and hugged me tighter. "I guess it

might be worse if she'd done all that without even caring that much about him."

She might have a point there, but it didn't make me feel much better. I sighed and nuzzled her hair, letting the citrusy scent of her shampoo fill my nose and soothe my nerves a little.

"That's not even the worst thing," I mumbled.

Maddie pressed a kiss to my cheek. "Do you want to talk about the worst thing or just forget about it?"

"I don't think I can forget." I heaved a breath. "I already hated that someone died while I got my second chance. And now it turns out it was probably at the expense of someone who didn't even *want* to donate their liver. Someone who was forced into it or maybe even killed so their organs could be taken and sold to save my life."

Maddie gazed up at me, her dark blue eyes full of perfect certainty. "But none of that is your fault. You didn't have any choice in it. Nothing you did then or now could have stopped it from happening. You know that, right?"

"I do," I said, but my shoulders sagged again. "It still feels like shit."

And as wrapped up as I was in Doom's Seed's crimes, the stolen organ inside me wasn't even much use as evidence after how well the bastard had covered his tracks.

How the hell were we going to bring him down?

CHAPTER
ELEVEN

Madelyn

S ummer shook her head dismissively before her smile shone from my phone's screen, lifting my spirits. "It's not like it matters where he got it from. I realize I've been hard on Logan, but even *I* know that no one could blame him for what his mom and that creepy crime boss did."

I sighed and leaned back in the chair across from the side table where I'd propped up my phone for our video chat. "But it matters to him anyway. Someone could have been killed for him to get that liver, so I get why it's hard for him to accept the situation. The really scary thing, though, is how far this reaches. We've found a few dozen recipients just in this city and the nearby areas. We think Doom's Seed has been running the business farther abroad than that."

"We're talking all over the state?" Summer asked, balling a couple of socks together. I'd caught her in the middle of a laundry session.

"Possibly the entire country—or even outside it."

My bestie paused in her laundry folding to gape at me. "Okay, that's just crazy. How can you guys think you'll take on this asshole on your own? No offense, but you're not equipped for this, Madds. I don't want to see any of you getting hurt—or even killed. And that includes even Logan."

I wrinkled my nose at the fact that she'd added him as an aside. "I know," I said. "But we aren't on our own now. Beckett and his people are doing a lot of the legwork, and they're on the same level as Doom's Seed. They know what they're doing."

"If you say so." Summer's gaze slid from my face to what she could see of the room beyond me. "He definitely has nice digs. I guess I could see hooking up with a criminal overlord if it comes with perks like that."

I mock-glowered at her. "I'm not with him for the perks. He's honestly got one of the strongest moral codes out of anyone I know. It's just... a little different from what we're used to. And you can believe he's doing whatever he can to protect me, even when I'd rather he did *less*."

"Well, I approve of that side of him, anyway."

Summer winked at me. Then her smile faltered. "You're sure you're not taking on too much?"

"I think I'm safer getting to the bottom of this mess and making sure the people behind it *can't* hurt us anymore than I am sticking my head in the sand and pretending it isn't happening."

"You might have a point there." Summer grimaced. "Which is why I still haven't told your parents what's up, no matter how pissed off they are with me. Your mom and Logan's dad pretty much hate me now, just so you know."

"I'm sure they don't hate you," I said. "They're just... frustrated. Which I get."

"And so do I. But they have to accept that I'm sticking with you, and if I trust you, they should too."

A weary smile crossed my face. Summer really was the best. A jab of guilt ran through my gut at the thought that I'd ever doubted her ability to handle the dangerous turn my life had taken.

"Has everything seemed normal on your end?" I had to ask.

My best friend nodded. "I've been keeping an eye out around school, but so far I haven't noticed anything or anyone sketchy. No sign that the boogie man is coming after me."

I restrained myself from rolling my eyes at her blasé tone. "And you've been taking extra precautions to keep safe?"

"Yeah, yeah. I never walk anywhere alone. I've got my mace, and I wear my whistle like a good girl."

"I'm not just being paranoid. They did go after my mom. It's not like it's a secret that you're my best friend."

Summer held up her hands. "I'm not complaining. It just feels a little weird, acting like I'm a target when nothing remotely abnormal has happened in this neck of the woods. How have you been handling *your* courses since you've been hiding away at your boyfriend's house?"

I rubbed my forehead, remembering the reading I'd been doing right before this call. "The guys and I all told our professors that we had family emergencies we had to go home for the week to deal with. I've been working through my assignments whenever I get the chance while I'm here."

"And if you need to be in hiding for more than a week?"

I shrugged. "I'm hoping it doesn't come to that, but if it does, we'll have to figure it out then. I don't like how this is interfering with my studies… but I'm definitely never becoming a doctor if I'm *dead.*"

"Very true. Keep remembering that." Summer shook a clothes hanger at the screen and then set it aside to pick up a tube of lipstick.

As she applied it, I raised my eyebrows. "What are you getting all dolled up for? Do you have a hot date you didn't tell me about?" The thought sent a twinge of panic through me—how well did she know the guy? Where would he take her?

Could she really trust him?

But Summer just laughed. "Oh, this is for a shift at the restaurant I said I'd cover tonight. The more makeup I wear, the better the tips. Some of us haven't found our rich sugar daddies yet, you know."

She grinned wide to show she was only joking, and I did let myself roll my eyes then.

At the same moment, Beckett pushed past the door to his rooms with an urgency that immediately set my nerves on edge. After one glance at his tensed posture and dark expression, I turned back to the phone. "It looks like I've got to get going. I'll update you when anything else comes up, like I promised. Be careful out there, all right."

"As you've only reminded me a gazillion times." She made an air kiss in my direction. "Don't worry about me, bestie."

As she ended the chat, I swiveled around to face Beckett. "What's wrong?"

The sound of my question was enough to draw the Vigil guys in from the small terrace off the sitting room, where they'd been taking a moment to relax while I talked with Summer.

Beckett's gaze swept over all of us. "Doom's Seed is at it again. Apparently he's taken the attitude that if he can't have something, no one can."

Logan had already been frowning, and the lines around his mouth deepened. "What do you mean?"

Beckett let out a ragged breath and started to pace across that end of the room. "Instead of attacking our properties, now he's outright destroying them. All across the city—so much of what we've worked for... What *I've* worked for..."

With a sound of frustration, he pulled out his phone and flipped to the photos. Walking over to us, he held it up.

A gasp broke from my lips as I recognized the dance club that he owned, the one where I'd gotten awfully up close and personal with the other guys more than once, now a blackened burned-out skeleton. The only reason I *could* recognize that charred frame as the club was because of the chunk of its sign that'd fallen to the ground with a few of the letters still visible.

"No," Slade muttered, his eyes flashing with anger.

Beckett swiped through to another picture and another. "The trucking company—with a bunch of the trucks still inside. An apartment building we own in the city. A department store we took on a few years ago."

Each of them was equally destroyed, wracked by fire and maybe even explosions to cause that level of damage. Nothing remained but broken walls and heaps of ash-covered rubble.

I winced even harder when he reached the last picture, full of shattered glass and scorched steel beams.

"The new office complex," Beckett said, his voice getting even rougher.

I knew what that place had meant to him, how much he'd been enjoying seeing his new venture come together—and all the good he'd meant to do with it too. Doom's Seed hadn't just destroyed the income Beckett's family would have made from it but also the pro bono medical clinic that'd been going to serve so many of the city's people in need.

"Fuck," Logan said hoarsely.

But then, maybe I shouldn't have been surprised. This was what Doom's Seed did, wasn't it? He took good things and ruined them.

"How did he manage to destroy so many locations so thoroughly?" Dexter asked, ever searching for details.

Beckett tucked his phone into his pocket. "All the fires were set overnight with copious amounts of gasoline to ensure they'd spread fast and be difficult to put out. And having so many large buildings go up in flames at the same time stretched the fire department thin, which made it even harder for them to deal with them all." His head drooped. "Most of the buildings were empty for the night, but the apartment building— not everyone made it out in time."

I swallowed thickly and stepped forward to grasp his arm. He leaned a little into my touch, so clearly anguished that I wished I knew how to erase all the horror that psychopath had dealt out.

How could Logan's mom believe she *loved* a man who'd do something like this?

Logan squared his shoulders, his tone hardening. "Should we go investigate the scenes? Try to turn up some evidence that could prove Doom's Seed was involved?"

Beckett shook his head. "My people are already checking for evidence of the perpetrators, but I doubt we'll find anything we could use. We've already seen how good Doom's Seed is at covering his tracks."

Dexter had perked up a bit at the prospect of taking action. "We might spot something they've missed. With a different perspective—"

Beckett held up his hand to stop the other guy. "I appreciate the sentiment, but I'm also concerned that this could be a trap. In the chaos, he could have people watching, looking for a chance to grab or kill any of you. It isn't worth the risk."

I winced. "You think he did all this just to set up a trap?"

"I don't know." Beckett pinched the bridge of his nose. "Mostly I think he just wanted to hit me in a way that would hurt. To get back at me as effectively as possible. I can't say he did a bad job of that."

No, because Doom's Seed had plenty of practice with those sorts of tactics too. A rush of chilly fear washed over me with the memory of Mom's car accident: the strange text that had warned me it might be fatal next time, the worried phone call from Holand, and then seeing her battered and bruised in the hospital bed...

My heart lurched, and I turned toward Beckett. "He might not stop with you. He's got to be pissed off that I escaped from Yvonne—and that Logan probably knows how he's involved in the organ business now too. What's to stop him from coming after everything we care about next? The *people* we care about?"

Logan's face turned sallow. "He did warn you about your mom."

I nodded, my heart starting to race. "He's switched back to personal attacks, and it's hard to believe he's going to draw the line at burning down buildings." I turned back to Beckett. "We've got to get them out. My and Logan's family and Summer—we have to bring them to a safe place before Doom's Seed targets them too."

CHAPTER
TWELVE

Madelyn

"How do you think they're going to take this?" Summer asked from the seat beside me as I pulled the big seven-seater SUV that Beckett had lent us into the driveway of my family home. With so much going on between his forces and Doom's Seed's, and with him being a stranger to my mom and stepdad, it hadn't made sense for him to join us on this mission, but he was joining us in spirit.

I glanced over at my bestie, who had her arms folded tight over her chest. *She* hadn't exactly taken my insistence that she needed to lay low for at least a few days super well, but she had come along with only a little arguing. But then, she'd already been aware of the dangerous situation I'd found myself in.

"We'll just have to give it our best shot and see how it goes," I said, squaring my shoulders, and looked back at the guys in the row behind us. "Ready?"

Slade gave me a cheeky salute that was offset by his somber expression, and Logan nodded before yanking open the door.

Dexter caught my gaze for just an instant in his usual fleeting way. "We'll back you and Logan up, however much of the story you feel you need to tell them."

"Same," Summer said emphatically, clambering out. "If you think the situation is serious enough that you're willing to spill the beans to them now, then they'd *better* listen."

Mom's and Holand's cars were parked farther down the driveway ahead of the SUV, so I knew they were home. I used my key in the door and eased it open, raising my voice to call down the front hall. "Mom?"

As the others filed in behind me, it was Holand who appeared first at the far end of the hall. He took us all in with a puzzled expression that turned sterner than I was used to. "We weren't expecting all of you. Not that it isn't good to see you after... everything." His gaze paused on me before sliding to his son. "What's going on, Logan?"

I dragged in a breath, letting the familiar faded floral scent that always filled my childhood home settle my nerves as much as anything could. "This was my idea."

"But I agree with her," Logan said right away, just as my mom appeared at the top of the stairs.

She walked down to them to join us, looking as confused and concerned as Holand. "Agree about what?" she said, and then couldn't seem to restrain herself from moving straight to me.

She pulled me into a tight hug. Her voice came out both choked and chiding. "You shouldn't have run off on us like that before. I've been so worried." She stepped back and looked all of us over, lingering on me the longest. "You are okay, aren't you?"

My mouth twisted. "In the most immediate sense. But we're not here for us. We came because I'm—we're—worried about the two of you."

Holand's brow furrowed. "What are you talking about? We've been perfectly fine. It's you two who've gone so quiet, refusing calls…" He trailed off, sounding as if he'd reined in his temper before he let loose more frustration than he'd prefer.

An ache formed in my gut. I hadn't wanted to put the two of them through so much stress, and I doubted Logan had either. This situation had spiraled out of our control so quickly.

"I know," I said. "And you have no idea how sorry we are about that. But that's why we came—because it's time we started telling you what's going on and made sure it isn't going to affect you any more than it already has."

Now Mom was frowning. "I don't understand, honey. What does this have to do with us?"

My hands twisted in front of me. Part of me wished we could be sitting comfortably in the living room, easing into this conversation—but there was never going to be anything comfortable about what I had to say. It was better to get it over with as quickly as possible so we could get our parents to safety quickly too.

"The truth is that we've made some very dangerous people angry," I said, beginning with the vaguest possible version of the story. The fewer details we had to get into, the less room there'd be for doubt and argument. "And those people are out to punish us however they can, including targeting the people we care about."

Mom blanched. "What do you mean? Is this something to do with drugs?"

I could have laughed if it hadn't been so much worse. "No, Mom, nothing like that. We haven't done anything wrong, but we stumbled on something that people with a lot of power and bad intentions didn't want us to know about, and now they're trying to keep us quiet."

"Then you need to go to the police," Holand broke in.

"We don't have enough proof," Logan said. "Believe me, we wish we could."

I caught Mom's gaze. "They've already caused your car accident. They texted me to tell me the next time they might kill you. I was hoping we could get them to forget about us, but it's become obvious that's impossible."

"My accident," Mom said, staring at me. "But—that *was* an accident."

I shook my head. "It was set up as a warning to us—to me."

"This sounds ridiculous, Maddie. If it's something that serious, we need to go down to the police station—"

"There's nothing to tell them!" I interrupted. "Just like Logan said. We've been trying to put together the evidence, but these criminals are very good at what they do. Which is why they're so dangerous."

"They're telling the truth," Summer piped up. "That's why I let Maddie make a run for it during the whole intervention thing. She explained it to me—she knows what she's talking about, Ms. Silver."

My mom's eyes widened. "You knew all about this too?"

"Only since the intervention," I said.

Holand's gaze fixed on Slade and Dexter. "And you boys are part of this scenario as well?"

"Unfortunately," Slade said with a crooked smile. "We've been right in the middle of it from the start."

"And why exactly are you telling us now?"

I swallowed hard. "Because we're worried that the people we're dealing with are going to go on the attack again, and Logan and I want to make sure you're safe. We're going to bring the two of you and Summer to someplace they won't know where to find you until they've been arrested." Or whatever else we or Beckett ended up having to do to ensure Doom's Seed was no longer a threat.

"You want us to take off in the middle of the week, dropping everything, to go to some unknown location?" Mom burst out. "Maddie, this is beyond anything I could have imagined. None of this makes sense. Who's been feeding you these stories? How did you get these crazy ideas in your head?"

My throat tightened even more. "It's not crazy, Mom. It's—" God, I hadn't wanted to tell her like this, but I didn't know what else to try. She wasn't going to budge until she knew what was actually at stake.

I drew up my chin and fixed her and Holand with the firmest look I could. "You know I've been asking about Dad more lately, and stopping by the hospital where he worked. It wasn't just because of the accident. We found information that makes it clear that Dad didn't die because of some mysterious illness. He was *murdered* because he found out about these people and the crimes they're committing. And while we were trying to find enough evidence to get justice for him, we caught their attention too."

I hadn't thought Mom's face could get any paler, but I was wrong. Her legs wobbled, and Holand slipped an arm around her waist.

"Your father—honey—the doctors said—" she mumbled.

"I know what they said—they never figured out what the cause was. We know for sure that he was murdered. We've heard it directly from these people. That's why they're trying to silence us by any means necessary."

Yvonne had confirmed it on the phone with Logan. But I didn't bring up that part because her presence was Logan's part of the story to tell. I doubted he wanted to dump the revelation that his mom was still alive on his dad right now like this, especially when that would only make our story sound crazier. I'd let him decide when the time was right for that discussion.

"I never wanted to tell you like this," I said to Mom, stepping closer to grasp her hand. "I swear that it's true, though. I can talk you through what we've found out—but that'll take time, and I don't know if these people will have already noticed we've come by the house. We need to get you to safety, and then we can deal with the rest."

"It's absolutely true," Dexter put in with his usual matter-of-fact tone. "I wouldn't get caught up in a mystery if the pieces didn't add up."

"We've been building our case for years," Slade said. "But just in the last few months, everything's started to unravel so fast."

For several seconds, Mom and Holand just stared at us. Then Holand asked in a low voice, "Where exactly do you want us to go?"

"We've made a friend who has experience with criminals like this," I said. "There's a vacant condo in a building he owns just an hour's drive from here. It'll be like a little vacation. Hopefully a short one."

Mom inhaled raggedly. "This is all so—I don't know what to think."

I squeezed her hand. "Please. Just come with us. Take a look at the place. Listen to what we have to say. And if you're absolutely sure you can't believe us, you can always come back. But I really hope you won't do that, because these people won't stop at anything to cover their tracks. And for them, that means destroying everyone connected to their crimes, which includes us too."

That last statement seemed to finally sink in enough for my mom to shake herself into action. She swiped at her eyes. "All right. We can call in sick for the next couple of days if it seems necessary. I want to hear the full story as soon as we get to this condo, though."

"Yes," Holand said firmly. "No more dodging around the truth. We can't trust you if you're not trusting us with all the details of what you claim is going on."

I nodded, gratitude rushing through me. "I understand. Why don't you pack a bag as fast as you can, and we'll get on to that part right after we get you settled in."

Mom turned toward the stairs as if in a daze, but not before she shot me one last look, as if she were staring at someone she no longer knew. My heart sank.

Please, let her understand eventually. I had no idea how I could have done things differently before that would have turned out better, but I didn't want to lose her.

———

The city lights glowed through the deepening night beyond the windows of the condo's main bedroom. The place was a penthouse, and the cars cruising by below looked no larger than fireflies.

Mom and I had come in here after the Vigil guys and I had laid out our entire case, other than the parts about Logan's mom. Logan had gone off to the side with his dad too. I'd thought Mom had wanted to talk, but for the first few minutes, she'd stayed silent, as if she were still absorbing everything.

I couldn't blame her for needing extra time to do that.

"We're definitely safe from this gang boss here?" she said finally.

The question reassured me a little—it told me she was taking the situation at least somewhat seriously.

"It's the safest place we can put you," I said. "There shouldn't be any way for his people to figure out you're here, as long as you stay inside and don't use your credit card for anything. Or place any calls on your usual phones. We'll leave you with the burner phone and credit card I showed you, and you can use those for anything you need while you're here."

The building was owned by Beckett's family through a few layers of shell companies, so it was unlikely Doom's Seed would even realize it was connected to him, let alone that we'd brought Mom, Holand, and Summer here. A few of Beckett's people had been watching when we'd driven off and checked out the area enough to confirm that no one malicious had followed us.

"And you're sure this friend of yours has our best interests at heart?"

I hadn't explained the full details of my relationship with Beckett to her either. I figured we could ease into that later. "Yes. He's gone above and beyond for all of us more than once."

Mom sighed. "I suppose I can understand now why you and Logan have been acting so strangely. It was all because of what you'd found out about your dad?"

"That's all of it," I said. "I hope you can see why I hesitated to tell you… It *does* sound crazy if you haven't been right in the middle of it."

She rubbed her forehead. "I still wish you'd tried. Hearing it all at once—it's hard to wrap my head around it."

I could still hear a hint of doubt in her voice. She wasn't totally convinced that we weren't exaggerating the situation, imagining a murder where there was only an accident, turning a minor criminal who'd threatened us into a much bigger monster.

"I know, Mom. But even if you're still not totally sure what to believe, I hope you can believe me that *I'll* feel so much better if you take this little vacation. For me and Logan, so we don't have to worry about you. If it turns out there's nothing *to* worry about, then we'll get whatever help we need to. But right now, all that matters is knowing you'll be okay." I paused. "I don't want them getting to you like they did to Dad."

"It sounds like something out of a movie, you know. Illegal organ transplants, covert investigations." Mom shook her head. "I suppose your father was acting a little secretive in those last few months before he died, now that I think about it. Not in a way that worried me at all, just like he was a bit busier at work than usual, and he hadn't told me what he was working on. But he often had confidential projects."

"He's a hero," I said gently. "If it wasn't for him, we'd never have stumbled on this either. Because he did, we might be able to stop so many more people from being hurt."

She leaned back with her hands on the mattress. "That does sound like him too. Always wanting to protect people in his own way. Usually he did it with his medical knowledge... but I could see him getting tangled up in a mystery like this."

"He was trying to protect us too by keeping us out of it," I had to point out.

"I know." Her gaze darted to me. "I'm not sure you aren't being a little overprotective. Nothing about my accident seemed unusual—to me or the doctors. But... it can't *hurt* to take a little time off and ease your worries. We'll figure this whole thing out together, honey. I know we will."

I beamed at her, tears prickling behind my eyes. Mom held out her arms, and I met her hug halfway.

This was the most I could have asked for. As long as

she was out of harm's way, we could see the rest of our mission through.

I could keep fighting for both of us—for us and for Dad.

A wordless shout of shock from beyond the door had my head jerking up. A second later, Logan's voice called out. "Maddie, you'd better get in here."

Mom hurried behind me as I pushed out into the condo's living room. The guys were gathered on the sofa facing the TV, Holand standing behind the sofa, his jaw gone slack. Summer dashed out of the second bedroom where she'd been getting her stuff organized for the stay and stalled in her tracks when she caught sight of the scene.

I rushed over to the side of the sofa where I could see the TV too—and froze with a lurch of my stomach.

They'd brought up the local news channel from back home. On the screen, a news anchor motioned toward a house behind him, lit up by the flames that were raging all through the building while firefighters swung their hoses toward it. "No one is sure what started the fire, but so far it's defied the firefighters' attempts to douse it."

I missed the rest of what she said as horror seared through my thoughts.

I knew that house. I knew the tree out front and the design on the awning over the porch. I knew the stones forming the path up to the porch steps.

I'd been at that house just a couple of hours ago. It was my family home that was burning.

CHAPTER
THIRTEEN

Madelyn

I'd never walked so cautiously through the house where I'd lived almost my entire life.

The place was a blackened shell of what it'd once been. The foundation stood mostly intact, walls and floors where they should be, but even those surfaces were so charred that I tested each patch of floor before putting my weight on it.

Technically it wasn't safe for me to be exploring the ruin at all, but I hadn't been able to stand the thought of losing one last visit to my former home. To see exactly how much Doom's Seed had destroyed.

The answer was pretty much everything.

Nothing remained of the furniture except the barest of bones: a few chunks of the sofa's frame, the scorched appliances with melted dials. Everything smaller and flammable had transformed into indistinguishable heaps of coals and ashes.

It felt as if I'd stepped into some alternate dimension where my hometown was a warzone. This couldn't *really* be my house in the world I actually lived in, could it?

But I hadn't hopped across any dimensions. The war we were fighting was all too real and happening right here around me. As the other people in the house with me were a stark reminder of.

Beckett glanced over at me when I raised my head. He'd been staying within arm's reach the entire time, as if he thought he might need to yank me to safety at any moment. Also toward that purpose, he had a few men stationed outside the building, watching for any sign of enemy forces.

Logan stood several feet away in what remained of the dining room. He was staring at the place where the table had once been, his hands clenched at his sides, maybe remembering the family dinners we'd enjoyed there during the short time he and I had shared this home. Slade and Dexter waited nearby, tensed and apprehensive, their gazes flicking between their best friend and me.

When Slade caught my gaze now, I gave him a slight nod to say I was hanging in there. Logan needed support too.

"I can tell it was a beautiful house," Beckett said quietly, reaching out to rub my shoulder.

I nodded, fighting the burn of tears behind my eyes. "Yeah. I couldn't have asked for a better place to grow up."

"I'm so sorry. I got you dragged into a war between two immense syndicates… I never would have wanted you—or anyone else outside of my world—getting caught in the crossfire like this."

The guilt in his words tugged at my heart. "It's not your fault," I said without hesitation. "This might have happened even if we'd never met. It was me joining up with the Vigil's investigation into my dad's death that put me on Doom's Seed's radar and made him want to scare me off." A rough laugh caught in my throat. "Maybe I should be apologizing to you for dragging you into *our* war."

Beckett let out a dismissive sound. "Doom's Seed must have had plans to move on my territory regardless. He just happened to be able to combine two of his goals. And connecting you to me probably made him even more determined to hurt you."

I exhaled in a rush. "At least I got Mom and Holand out in time. The house is just a thing. The people are what's really important." The laugh finally worked its way out of my mouth, but it didn't have much humor in it. "And now Mom totally believes that the danger I was trying to convince her about is real."

"Always looking on the bright side." Beckett stepped close enough to press a gentle kiss to my temple.

I was trying to stay optimistic, anyway. I'd said the

house was only a thing, but I knew it was more than that. It was memories. It was a sense of belonging.

It'd held so many of my lingering impressions of Dad, and those were now burned up along with the furnishings.

Here in the living room, he would spread out the props for a scientific experiment on the coffee table and help me arrange them so we could complete a test of magnetism or kinetic force. Anything biological or chemical, of course, had to be in the kitchen because of the potential for mess. I could remember Mom standing in the doorway, shaking her head with a bemused smile, as I sent a wooden car careening off the table to bang into the baseboard.

So many times, we'd curled up on the sofa that was now ashes to watch one of the animated flicks I'd loved at that age, which Dad had always acted completely absorbed in even though he must have gotten bored to tears. He'd make popcorn fresh in the pan and douse it with so much melted butter it'd leave a sheen on our fingers.

I could almost taste the salty flavor I'd lick off my fingertips when the popcorn was gone.

How long would it take before those memories started to fade without the surroundings to remind me?

I swallowed thickly and turned toward the staircase. It was intact too but badly burnt. I crept over to it and treaded up it with even more care than I'd approached the floor downstairs. Beckett followed a couple of steps behind.

The banister had mostly crumbled away. I stuck close to the wall, edging along it to the door to my bedroom. The room I'd expected to come back to during the summer if I didn't get a position in the city that kept me there.

My wrought-iron bedframe looked almost the same as it always had, just blacker. And everything else was burnt black too, drifts of cinders rolling across the floor like dusty hills. My throat closed up.

All the nights I'd lain on that bed daydreaming about boys… most often Logan. All the assignments I'd completed sitting at the desk that was now nothing but dead embers. The posters I'd left on the walls, a little childish—a band I'd loved in tenth grade, an inspirational poster I'd gotten in junior high that was maybe a little saccharine—but *mine*.

Gone. All of it gone.

I dragged my gaze away and ventured farther down the hall. The door at the end opened up to what had once been Dad's office.

Mom had started using it herself, but she'd kept the big oak desk and the bookshelves lining every possible inch of wall, most of them still packed with his old texts and reference manuals. "You'll want your pick of them someday when you get that medical degree," she'd used to say to me.

Now every scrap of paper had been eaten up in the flames.

In the back of my mind, I could see the desk where it had once stood, with the trinket box I'd held on to perched by the corner. Dad leaning back in his chair behind it, smiling at me when I'd darted in to ask him a question. Motioning me over to show me some video or computer-generated model he'd brought up on his laptop. Hugging me close while he explained the concepts with perfect patience.

I blinked hard and pulled myself away. My fingers had turned black from touching the walls for balance. I couldn't even wipe at my eyes without smudging my face.

An ache filled my chest, but there wasn't anything I could do about it. No way to deny or reverse the damage in front of me.

I turned around and headed back to the staircase, Beckett following suit and glancing at me over his shoulder to make sure I kept coming.

My heart was so heavy that it seemed to drag me down the steps. I found the Vigil guys standing in the living room when I reached the front hall, all their expressions grim. Slade motioned me over and pulled me into an embrace.

"It was a big price to pay," he said in an unusually rough voice. "You shouldn't have been the one who had to pay it."

"It was Logan's house too," I said, turning my head against Slade's chest to study my stepbrother.

His mouth stayed tense and slanted, but he shrugged. "I lived here for less than two years. I liked the place, but I know I don't have anywhere near the same kind of connection to it that you do. I'm so sorry, Maddie."

Dexter held up his phone. "I took pictures in case there's anything we need for evidence—or for remembrance's sake—later."

I shot him a tight smile. "Thank you."

As I eased away from Slade and took in the devastation around me again, a stronger swell of grief and melancholy swept over me.

Had our quest to find Dad's killer really been worth it when I'd ended up losing all this? It'd been Mom and Holand's home as well. All the trappings that'd propped up so many memories, all the security and comfort this home had offered… So much we could never get back. And even if we could see justice done and Doom's Seed punished for his crimes, that wouldn't bring the house or Dad back.

Those thoughts ran through my head, and a spurt of anger flared up inside my chest. This was all that asshole's fault. He'd stolen Dad from us, and then he'd hurt Mom, and now he'd destroyed our home as well.

How much more would he get away with if we *didn't* keep fighting him?

If it hadn't been my life he was messing up, it would have been someone else's. No doubt it already was hundreds of other people's at the same time, with all his malicious business practices. And lots of those people weren't in any position to fight back themselves.

We'd set out on this crusade because it was right and because we could. Neither of those facts had changed.

Backing down and giving up was exactly what Doom's Seed would have hoped would happen when I was faced with his latest vicious act.

My jaw set. I was never going to give him the satisfaction.

His reign of terror had to end, and we were the ones closest to doing it. So we had to see it through before he destroyed even more lives.

I looked around at each of the guys, squaring my shoulders. "It doesn't matter how much I lost. We aren't backing down. All this means is that we need to get on with stopping Doom's Seed once and for all."

CHAPTER
FOURTEEN

Madelyn

Dexter moved around the mansion's kitchen like a storm. He'd sent Slade on a shopping trip to gather all the ingredients he needed to make some kind of elaborate meal for us. I knew, though, that the meal was mainly for me—to get my spirits up after what I'd just witnessed.

I wanted the gesture to work, but I was so wiped out. Images from the burned house kept wavering through my mind.

I'd come over to the kitchen island to offer to help, but Dexter was too busy ordering Logan and Slade around to give me any instructions. After he'd gotten Logan chopping one thing and Slade grating another, he finally looked at me.

"This is going to take a while," he said. "Why don't you get some rest? We'll let you know when it's time to eat."

I wanted to protest, but it was hard to summon enough resolve. It wasn't as if Dexter couldn't handle himself in a kitchen. I wasn't sure I'd actually contribute rather than ruining the ingredients.

Beckett, who'd been watching over the proceedings with a vaguely bemused expression, slipped his hand around my elbow. "I'll come with you. It's been a long day—you need a break."

"Fine," I muttered, but I couldn't deny I felt a little relief being escorted up the stairs and toward his private apartment. I didn't even want to sleep—just to lie down and take the weight off my feet even if I couldn't remove the heavy burden pressing down on my shoulders.

Beckett didn't bring me to the guestroom where I'd spent the previous night. Instead, he led me right into his part of the house to his own private bedroom.

I sank down on the bed, still upright, with the sense that he'd wanted to do more than make sure I got to a resting spot safely. Beckett sat at the edge of the mattress and turned to face me. His expression had turned so solemn that my heart lurched.

"What's wrong?" I asked.

Beckett shook his head. "Nothing—not like that. I just—you know what you said at your house, about stopping Doom's Seed?"

"Of course. I mean, obviously we have to."

"*I* have to." He reached out and grasped both my

hands. "Maddie, I'm aware that you meant every word, but I want you to listen to me. You should walk away. This is my fight now, against people I was at least partly prepared to go up against. You've been through so much already—I don't want to see you lose anything more."

I frowned at him. "I'm okay. I can handle this. Seeing my house burned down was a shock, but that doesn't mean—"

He squeezed my hands to stop me. "I'm not saying this because I think you can't do enough. I just want you to let me handle the risks from here on out. I'm in a way better position to cope. I swear to you, I'll put everything I have toward crushing Doom's Seed. You won't need to worry about him hurting you or the people you care about again."

My voice softened. "I'll have to worry about him hurting *you*."

"That's going to be the case either way." Beckett held my gaze, his cool gray eyes fiercely determined. "Please, Maddie. Let me do this for you."

My heart fluttered at the passionate devotion in his words. He really would do it—fight this entire battle on his own, on my behalf as well as his. The flare of protective furor in his eyes set off an answering heat low in my belly, stirring me out of my melancholy daze in a way nothing else had.

"Beckett, you know what I have to say," I said, gently but firmly. "I'm as committed as you are to seeing Doom's Seed fall. I *want* to have a hand in taking down the asshole who ripped so much away from me—I want to know I got justice for my family myself, not just sitting on the sidelines while someone else did the work."

Beckett's jaw tightened. "You've already done a lot to get us to this point. You've hardly been on the sidelines."

"And I'm not going there now. I'm not letting you take all the responsibility after we've come so far." I got up on my knees so I could look down at him rather than the other way around and rested my hand on his shoulder. "I'm strong enough to stand beside you while we fight this battle. That's the only place I want to be."

To emphasize those words, I gave him a push, and Beckett didn't resist. I shoved him right down on the bed and pressed my mouth to his.

This kiss wasn't gentle or sweet the way I might have kissed any of the guys before. I melded my lips to his with all the strength and desire I had in me.

He needed to remember that I was so much more than a victim, that I could take charge even with a man as powerful as him.

I ran my hands down his chest as I kissed him again. Beckett tangled one hand in my hair and trailed the other down my side to my hip, returning the kiss fervently but letting me stay in control.

I eased back just enough to peer down at him, pinning him with my gaze. "I'm capable of fighting my own battles when I need to. I'm strong enough to take on whatever enemies come my way. I don't *need* you to take the reins, as much as I appreciate your help."

He smiled up at me. "You already have that."

"Good."

I slammed my mouth into his again, need swelling through my body and condensing at my core. When Beckett squeezed my ass, I couldn't help grinding against him through our clothes. He groaned against my mouth, and I devoured the sound with a whimper of my own, feeling the bulge that had already hardened behind his fly.

I could take whatever the world threw at me—and I could take him. I curled my fingers into his hair, rumpling the neat strands, and yanked his head back so I could claim his neck with my mouth as well.

When I nipped him with the tips of my teeth, he let out another groan, massaging my ass. "I think I like this. I should try to take over more often, just to see what comes out of you."

"No, you definitely should not," I muttered against his throat, and flicked my tongue across it. The hitch of his breath made me giddy.

I slid my hand down his torso to the hem of his buttoned shirt and tugged it upward. When it caught on his chest, I fumbled with the buttons between increasingly wild kisses. Beckett leaned upward to let me pull the shirt right off him and then reached for my own. I swatted his hands away with a sly smile and peeled it off myself, swaying over him.

"You're so fucking sexy," Beckett murmured, brushing his fingertips up my bare sides. I shivered eagerly at the contact and dove back in for another kiss.

This time, I trailed my lips down his neck and over his chest. Beckett stroked his fingers over my shoulders and into my hair, across my scalp, his breaths turning more ragged by the second. I flicked my tongue across one of his nipples and then delved my hand between us to cup the hardness I'd enjoyed so much against my pussy.

Beckett mumbled a swear word, his hips arching up to meet my grasp. He pumped into my hand through his slacks. I'd swear I felt his cock twitch when I swiveled my thumb over the head.

There was something so intoxicating about seeing this powerful, controlled man unravel under me at my attentions.

I needed more. I popped open the button of his fly, but when I gripped the zipper, Beckett caught my hand. He pushed himself up on his elbows, blinking the haze of pleasure from his eyes so he could hold my gaze.

"Maddie," he said, his voice steady if a bit rough, "I just need to know. Why does it matter so much to you to keep fighting when you don't have to? Why is it worth the risk?"

I paused, letting the question sink in. My answer rose up in my mind without any effort at all.

Dad had believed in me so much—but I'd fallen apart when he'd died. It'd taken years to get that inner strength back, but once I had, I knew he'd have been proud of all the causes I'd championed.

It was who I'd always wanted to be. Who I was meant to be, and no one was taking that away from me.

"There are only so many people in the world who are in a position not just to look after their own needs but also to try to make the world better for other people too," I said, measuring out the words as they came to me to make sure they felt right. "And for now, one of those people is me, so I'm going to do everything I can. Saving people who can't save themselves was always my goal with my medical career. Taking down Doom's Seed and stopping him from hurting any more innocents isn't any different."

A soft smile curled Beckett's lips. He raised his hand to my cheek and stroked his thumb over my skin. Awe shone from his eyes.

"Every time I think I couldn't admire you more, you prove me wrong. You absolutely can hold your own alongside me, Maddie. And I want you there. I love you."

My pulse stuttered. He'd never said those three words before. Somehow I hadn't expected them, even though he'd made his devotion clear in so many other ways. I hadn't known if he'd want to admit a feeling that vulnerable.

But he was willing to offer up that much of himself to me. Only to me.

My throat tightened with a swell of affection before I propelled the words out. "I love you too. So much. For your strength, for how much *you* care, despite the kind of world you grew up in."

Beckett pulled me into a kiss, one that stretched on and on until my head was spinning. But I didn't plan on letting him take over this encounter, not like that.

I intended to demonstrate my love in all kinds of ways.

This time, when I yanked down the zipper on his slacks, he didn't move to stop me. I wiggled his pants and boxers down his hips so his rigid cock sprang free, thick and already beaded with precum. I licked my lips.

"That's right," Beckett said in a husky tone. "You can take all of that too. My fierce warrior."

An eager shiver passed through my body. I wrapped my hand around the base of his shaft and sucked him into my mouth.

Beckett's hips jerked. He gripped my hair again, pumping up to meet the movements of my mouth but holding himself back from ramming his cock right down my throat. I swiveled my tongue around him and teased my fingers over his balls, drawing a strained grunt out of him. His salty, musky flavor filled my senses.

"Fuck, Maddie," he rasped. "The things you can do with that mouth... But I want to be inside you properly. I want to hear you come apart around me with all that strength and fierceness."

Oh, God, I wanted that too. When he tugged at my hair, I allowed myself to lift off his cock and clamber over his body. Beckett yanked down my jeans and delved his hand between my legs. He inhaled sharply at the wetness already soaking my panties.

He twisted away from me for just a few seconds to

grab a packet out of the drawer on the bedside table. I snatched it from him and ripped it open, wanting to be a part of every piece of this act.

His eyes rolled back as I slid the condom down over his length. He gripped my hips but gave me the room to sink down over him at my own speed.

"Take me however you want," he murmured. "It's always so fucking good with you."

I took him in one inch at a time, whimpering at the thrilling stretch of his girth. When our hips met, I eased upward and plunged down again twice as fast.

Beckett's fingers dug into my thighs. As I set the tempo, he bucked up into me, sweat beading across his forehead.

The stretching sensation expanded into a deep fullness, which swelled into an ache for more. I rode him with every ounce of strength I had in me, taking him deeper and deeper, gasping with the pleasure of it.

I tipped my head back toward the ceiling, a moan tumbling out of me as Beckett thrust up into me with even more force than before. One of his hands slipped across my hip to settle over my pussy. His fingers flicked across my clit, and I pumped him into me faster, faster, bliss spiraling up inside me until I burst.

My orgasm crashed through me, jerking a cry from my lips and leaving me shuddering over one of the four incredible men I loved. My channel clamped around Beckett's cock, and he held me tight as he followed me over the edge with a choked sound of release.

"So goddamn good," he muttered, wrapping his

arms around me and pulling me down against him so our chests were perfectly aligned. "You're a fucking goddess, Maddie. Don't let anyone ever tell you differently, even me."

A soft chuckle escaped me. I nestled my head under his chin, drifting on the afterglow and soaking up the warmth of his naked body. In that moment, I never wanted to let him go.

A chilling thought prickled through me on the heels of my contentment. I pressed myself tighter against him, but I couldn't escape the icy edge of fear that had crept into my mind.

Beckett had talked about how much I'd already lost. What if Doom's Seed tried to take this happiness from me too?

How could I be sure he wouldn't succeed?

CHAPTER
FIFTEEN

Dexter

"I hate that we're always simply responding to his attacks, always on the defensive," Beckett muttered. "We need to get the upper hand—or at least take more control over the situation."

I glanced over at him where he was poised at the table in his sitting room with the others, digging into leftovers from last night's dinner. As much as I liked seeing them enjoying my food, I wanted to contribute more than that.

Which was why I'd moved over to the sofa on my own to concentrate on the data in front of me.

I yanked my gaze back to my list of the attacks Doom's Seed's people had made on us and Beckett so far. I'd noted down dates, time of day, locations, and the apparent motivation behind the assault: personal or strategic, aiming to claim or to destroy.

It all looked random at a glance, but I knew that people were rarely able to make their actions totally random unless they had complex computer systems involved. They might *think* they were mixing things up too much to be predictable, but a pattern would still emerge if you took in the big picture from the right angle.

Doom's Seed didn't want us to be able to predict where he'd strike next. He was trying to keep Beckett and the rest of us on our toes. But he wasn't impervious. No one was.

If I could make a good guess at where he'd launch his next attack, Beckett could focus his manpower there instead of waiting for his people to call in and scrambling to launch a defense.

It would be coming soon. Since the first full-out assault, Doom's Seed had rarely waited more than forty-eight hours before launching another of some sort, and usually it'd been closer to twenty-four.

I ran through the list again in my head, feeling out the rhythm of it. Inside the city and outside. Business-related or fear tactics. He kept looping around between all the different factors… and when I considered which he *hadn't* acted on recently, his next step suddenly seemed obvious.

A surge of hope raced through me, but I made myself examine the data again to double-check my instincts. If I sent us off on a wild goose chase, Beckett could end up worse off in the face of the next attack, not better.

When I was confident, I pushed myself to my feet. "I have an idea of where Doom's Seed will come at you next."

Beckett's head jerked up, and Madelyn and my friends focused on me as well, Madelyn offering me an encouraging smile.

"By all means, let's hear it," Beckett said, watching me with a thoughtful expression. I could hear the respect in his tone.

I'd better make sure I earned it.

"Making an educated guess," I said, "I believe that his next target will be a property of yours that has strategic value but is a little farther away from where most of the conflict has been—outside the city. Maybe pretty far outside. Something like the farm, where it was separate from your businesses around here but still could damage your family's reputation if you lost it."

Beckett's eyebrows rose. He rubbed his jaw as his gaze went distant with thought, and then his expression tightened. "If you're right, then I know exactly where he'll come gunning for us next. I don't have many men out there. I can call more in."

Logan pushed his plate away. "We should go out there too. It worked well when you rallied the troops at the farm. And the more hands on deck, the better."

Beckett hesitated for a second, his gaze sliding to Madelyn, but when she gave him a firm look, he nodded. "Let's go, then. If we get there before he has his people in place, he might even call off his plans."

We rushed out to the same van we'd taken out to the farm, although Beckett got in behind the wheel this time. He'd mentioned that his people in the area were being spread increasingly thin with so many casualties and injuries after the past attacks.

A sense of nervous exhilaration kept sweeping through me as the van roared out of the city along one of the freeways. Please, let me be right about this. If I was, then I'd given us a huge advantage.

If I wasn't, then I might have totally screwed our new friend over.

Maddie had taken the passenger seat next to Beckett. "Where exactly are we going?" she asked.

"My family owns an entertainment complex out here at the far edge of the suburbs," Beckett said. "We use it to launder most of our money from our less legitimate local activities. It's almost as far from the city proper as the farm, and it'd be a significant blow if something happened to it."

He turned the wheel to veer down an exit ramp. I twisted on the bench to peer out the side window.

"It's just up ahead," Beckett said, and his phone's ringtone started pealing. He fished it out of his pocket while holding on to the steering wheel with his other hand and glanced at the call display. A frown darkened his expression. "It's one of my men who was stationed out there—I talked to him less than an hour ago when we left."

He hit the speaker phone button and set the phone down in the cup holder slot. "What's going on, Matt?"

At the same moment, gunfire boomed through the air—fainter through the windows and louder as it crackled from the gun's speakers. My stomach plummeted. Before the man even spoke, I knew what'd happened.

I'd been right—but I'd figured it out too late.

"The pricks just swarmed us," the guy on the other end of the phone hollered. "How far away are those reinforcements? Fuck."

More shots reverberated through the speaker. Beckett spat out a curse and slammed his foot down on the gas. "We're just a couple of blocks away, and the others should be right on our tail!"

He blew through a stop sign without a hint of concern and careened into the huge parking lot around an expansive entertainment center. Movie posters lined the wall of the cinema that bulged from this corner of the building.

But the people who'd come to enjoy those movies and everything else the complex had to offer weren't getting much entertainment right now. Shrieks and cries carried through the air as we screeched to a halt at the edge of the parking lot. Only a little relief flashed through me at the sight of three more cars tearing around the bend to follow us.

We were going to need all the help we could get. Beckett leapt out, and we did the same, but we stayed braced behind the doors to use them as shields as we took in the scene before us.

At least twenty figures waving guns were spread out across the parking lot close to the complex. Several of them were taking shots at the outside of the building, shattering a window here, smashing a store sign there. Others yelled at patrons who were now fleeing toward their cars.

They weren't killing those innocents—not yet, anyway—but they were doing their best to terrify them.

"Don't let us see your faces around here again!" one shouted loud enough for me to hear over the gunfire. "And tell your friends to stay away too."

Beckett sucked in a ragged breath. "They want word to get around that this happened—that it'd be dangerous to come here. Dry up all our business. Fucking assholes."

"Not just that," Slade said with an anxious note in his voice. "I think those guys right by the building have gasoline cans."

I squinted through the dimming evening light and realized it was true. Three figures were splashing liquid from what looked like gas cans against the walls of the complex.

They were planning to burn down even more of Beckett's business. Scaring off his customers was just a side benefit. And it meant that even if we stopped the fire in time, they'd already caused plenty of damage.

The other cars skidded to a halt around us. Men

poured out of them, and Beckett hollered to them with a wave of his hand.

The attackers around the building looked our way and fired several more shots at the building before swiveling around. But they didn't even try to take us down. They dashed toward the vehicles they must have arrived in.

All except two of the men with the gas cans, who paused just long enough to flick open lighters and toss them into two separate puddles of gasoline.

Flames hissed to life at the same time as our side opened fire. "Be careful of any pedestrians!" Beckett was urging, but as far as I could tell, all the ordinary people had already fled the scene. Thank God.

A couple of the attackers fell under the hail of bullets, but most dived into or between their cars in time. The fire roared up the two sides of the building like twin demons, ready to dig in their claws.

Beckett glanced between the retreating attackers and the building and appeared to decide that it wasn't worth going for revenge if his property went up in smoke in the meantime.

"Let them go!" he shouted. "Focus on putting out the fire!"

"With what?" one of his men hollered back.

A few of his people raced forward with bottles of water, but even I knew those weren't going to get very far. My mind spun with all the knowledge I'd accumulated across my life, and I whirled toward the spot where I could predict the water main would be located.

There'd be a hydrant somewhere along it… There!

"Over here!" I called out, running toward the yellow structure I'd caught sight of down the street. Several of Beckett's men followed me, but it must have only taken them a few seconds to figure out what I was after.

"Hold on! Get out of the way." One of them sprinted back toward his car.

The next thing I knew, the guy was speeding the car straight toward the hydrant. He slammed into it grill-first.

The hydrant burst, water spraying over the sidewalk as far as the edge of the parking lot. Well, I guessed that was one way to get it open.

A bunch of the men, as well as my friends and Madelyn, charged over to the hydrant. Everyone carried some sort of container, from the duffel bags that'd once held an assortment of weapons to bins and bags that'd been used for purposes I could only guess at. They held them up to the spewing water in turn and then raced toward the fire to toss the contents on the flames.

In the distance, I heard the first faint strains of fire-truck sirens. If we could just tame the fire a little, drown it as much as possible before the professionals arrived, maybe the damage would only be superficial.

A few of Beckett's people had remained by the cars, covering their colleagues with their gazes fixed on the retreating enemy. A handful of the attackers had paused by their cars to take shots at us, and Beckett's men returned fire without hesitation, determined to take down anyone they could.

My gaze caught on a man in that cluster of cars who was ducked down by the trunk of a sedan, his phone pressed to his ear. Was he talking to Doom's Seed right now?

He had to be speaking to someone important if he figured it was worth staying in the middle of a gunfight to find out what they had to say rather than racing off first.

"Hey!" I shouted at the men on our side who were closest to me, and gestured toward the guy who was mostly out of view. "We need to get our hands on that phone. It could lead us straight to the asshole behind this attack."

One of Beckett's men nodded and darted around the van to get a clearer shot. Just as the guy I'd spotted started to lower the phone, the man I'd called over squeezed the trigger.

The bullet caught our target in the wrist. With a yelp of agony, he jerked his arm toward him, blood spurting and the phone dropping from his fingers.

It clattered on the pavement. Beckett's people went back to firing at the last of the attackers, who were all scrambling into their cars now.

As they peeled away, I threw myself across the parking lot toward the fallen phone. I had to get to it before any of our enemies considered how valuable it could be and crushed it under a tire.

I kept my body low, hoping the men behind me

could fend off anyone who tried to shoot at me. A bullet whizzed by over my head, and my heart lurched. But I snatched up the phone and hurtled back the way I'd come, my pulse hammering away with a mix of elation and terror.

The sirens were blaring louder. Just as I leapt back into the shelter of the van, three fire trucks swerved into the parking lot. The firemen charged out and rushed to the hydrant, where thankfully Beckett's men had pulled the car out of range. Other firefighters started spraying down the building with water from the trucks' on-board tanks.

The flames started to sputter under the larger deluge of liquid. Doom's Seed's people hadn't been able to splash the gasoline all the way up the walls, and most of the fire sizzled out under the spray from the hoses. Black streaks cut through the pastel paint, but as far as I could tell, the flames hadn't eaten through the building to its contents.

Beckett was going to have a reconstruction project on his hands, but a much smaller one than it might have been if we hadn't headed out here when we had. His people's efforts with the hydrant had slowed the fire quite a bit.

At the moment, Beckett was waving to his men. In a matter of seconds, they'd jumped back into their cars while Beckett, Madelyn, and my friends scrambled into the van.

"The police will be here too, any minute now," Beckett said in explanation as we peeled out of the lot.

He drove in tense silence for several blocks before pulling over into a different parking lot outside a bingo parlor that was closed for the night. His breath came out in a ragged whoosh.

"We were too late," I said, my throat tightening. "I'm sorry."

"It's not your fault. It's that prick Doom's Seed," Beckett muttered. He sat up straighter, swiping his hand back through his hair. "You were right about the pattern. And it would have been worse if we hadn't been here. But business is still going to suffer a lot after the spectacle those pricks made. And having the cops sniffing around isn't great for us either."

"We stopped them from doing everything they wanted to," Madelyn insisted. "That's a partial win, anyway."

It occurred to me that in the panic of our departure I'd almost forgotten the one other possible win we'd made. I fished the confiscated phone out of my pocket. A smear of blood marked the screen, but it was otherwise undamaged.

I held it up. "We have this too. One of Doom's Seed's men was making a call on it in the parking lot— maybe getting instructions from the boss himself? Or someone else important. If he's the one who was getting the orders from people higher up, there could be some interesting material on there that we could use against Doom's Seed, right?"

Logan's eyes lit up. He gave me a thumbs up and took the phone from me. "That's brilliant, Dex."

Slade laughed. "Leave it to Dexter to find a way to turn a disaster around."

Even Beckett had perked up a little. He smiled at me with a tip of his head. "I saw you running over there —I didn't realize what for. Thanks for that. You really stuck your neck out."

"Anything I can do to help, I'm on it," I said, a strange sense of satisfaction washing over me.

I might not be immersed in the criminal underworld like Beckett's people, but I was a real part of this new, joint team we'd formed with him. I'd contributed in ways his men hadn't thought to on their own. Maybe hadn't even been capable of, when it came to recognizing the patterns.

And with the eager vibe that hummed between us as Logan turned on the phone and the rest of us looked on, we were becoming even more of a cohesive unit than we'd been before. Maybe even a family, with Madelyn right there at the center of it.

She caught my eye with one of her soft smiles, and I had to smile back. The family we'd formed wasn't just cohesive. It was the best one I could imagine.

CHAPTER
SIXTEEN

Madelyn

We pulled over to the curb next to a stretch of modest suburban houses, a few yards down from the specific house we were interested in. I peered at its pastel blue walls through the dim light from the streetlamps that'd blinked on with the descending night. A second car carrying the people Beckett had brought for backup parked behind us.

I dragged my gaze away from the house to glance at Logan in the seat next to mine. "You're sure this guy is connected to the illegal organ transplants?"

My stepbrother nodded. "The trail from the data we grabbed off that phone was clear enough once we dug far enough. And the guy's a doctor—Doom's Seed will obviously have needed some medical experts on board to make this work."

"We don't know exactly how connected Dr. Evancho is," Dexter piped up from where he was sitting next to Beckett up front. "It's possible he doesn't know the full extent of the situation."

"We'll approach him cautiously rather than aggressively." Beckett leaned forward to peer at the house. "I don't see any signs of a significant security system on the house."

At my other side, Slade tapped his window. "There's a car in the driveway. Someone's home."

I rubbed my arms, a chill passing through me despite the whir of the car's heater, and Logan set a reassuring hand on my shoulder. "It'll just be him. His one kid is grown up and lives in a totally different city now, and his wife's out of town this week speaking at a conference on the other side of the country. No innocent bystanders."

"Unless *he's* innocent," I pointed out.

"We'll figure that out," Beckett said confidently. "Let's go see what Dr. Steve Evancho will tell us, Maddie."

We all got out of the car, Beckett's men emerging from theirs as well, but everyone except Beckett and me hung back on the front lawn while the two of us climbed the steps. When we'd been hashing out the plan, I'd pointed out that seeing a young woman at the door might put the doctor a little more at ease than if he were faced with a bunch of tough-looking men.

The guys had only agreed because Beckett would be right there next to me—and fully armed, if things took a bad turn.

As Beckett pressed the button for the doorbell, my stomach knotted. I squared my shoulders and willed my nerves to settle, though my heart kept thumping on.

It was one thing to rush in to help in the middle of a fight already happening, when I could see there was an obvious threat. In this situation, for all intents and purposes, *we* were the threat. It wasn't a feeling I enjoyed.

The door eased open, revealing a man I knew from Logan's research was in his early sixties, with thin gray hair swept to the side of his broad forehead. At the sight of us, his eyes widened slightly while his jaw clenched.

He definitely didn't figure we were just canvasing for charity.

"Yes?" he said in a nervous tone.

"Dr. Evancho?" I said, and went on at the brief dip of his head, "We need to ask you about something important. I think you have information that could save a lot of lives."

His expression tightened even more, and he took a step back, his knuckles whitening where he gripped the door. "You must have the wrong person. I think you'd better leave."

"Please, Dr. Evancho," I started, but he cut me off.

"I have nothing to say to you—I don't know whatever you think it is I know. I'd appreciate it if you left my property right away."

He started to close the door, but Beckett caught it with a smack of his hand. He held the doctor's gaze with the cool fierceness I'd always admired in him, and lifted his shirt just enough to flash the gun in the concealed holster at his hip.

"We could get the police involved in this matter," he said firmly, "but we're willing to handle it privately, which I think is what you'd prefer. Especially considering who you're entangled with."

A flash of pure terror crossed Dr. Evancho's face, all but confirming our suspicions about his connection to Doom's Seed.

I held out my hand to him. "Please. We're not here to hurt you. We only want your help. I already—I lost my dad because of the people you've worked with. You've got to know that what's happening is wrong. Don't you want to see it stopped?"

"I don't know what you're talking about," the doctor muttered again, but he shifted his weight, not trying to force the door.

"You went through all that medical training," I tried again. "You dedicated your life to saving other people's lives. I can't believe you'd want to let innocents keep dying if you have the chance to end the suffering. What did you take that oath for?"

His mouth twisted. His gaze lifted to meet mine. We stared at each other in silence for a long moment.

"No one needs to find out you told us anything," Beckett put in. "We're not going to spread the word. And if we have our way, the only people who'd retaliate will be out of the picture soon regardless."

I wasn't sure which of us convinced him more, but after another several seconds of hesitation, Dr. Evancho sighed. He stepped back. "Fine. Come inside, but please, let's make this quick."

"Nothing would make me happier," Beckett said. "But I hope you'll understand that we have some company just to make sure we *all* stay safe."

A couple of his people lingered in the shadows around the house to keep watch. Three others trooped inside along with me, Beckett, and the Vigil guys. The doctor led us into the living room just beyond the front hall. As soon as he stopped, Beckett's three men gathered around him with menacing glowers.

Dr. Evancho cringed. "Don't hurt me. I'm cooperating. I—I never even wanted to be a part of this. I'm not some criminal mastermind."

Beckett eyed him, folding his arms over his chest. "Let's make sure we're talking about the same thing. What didn't you want to be a part of?"

The doctor's eyes flicked over all of us. "The—the organ transplants. That's what you're here about, isn't it? I can't imagine what else—"

He fell silent at Logan's nod.

"How did the man who brought you on make you get involved if you didn't want to be?" Dexter asked.

Dr. Evancho wrung his hands in front of him. "It

was under duress. I made a mistake when I was a lot younger than I am now, when I'd first started out at my practice. He took advantage of my lapse."

Slade raised his eyebrows. "What kind of mistake?"

The doctor looked away. "I skimmed some money out of the clinic. I didn't think anyone would realize, but the wrong people found out and used it to threaten me. If I hadn't done what they asked, they'd have exposed the crime, ruined me and my ability to provide for my family—my son was only a baby…"

I was torn between sympathy and revulsion that he'd let his initial weakness propel him into a much greater crime. "You helped with the transplant operations and—"

"No," Dr. Evancho broke in urgently. "No, I never touched a single patient, I swear it. I wouldn't have let it go that far. I only—they asked me to help them falsify records to cover for the patients they'd taken on. That's it. Just paperwork."

Just paperwork. Paperwork that'd helped cover up hundreds, maybe even thousands of organs illegally obtained and transplanted over the years. That'd allowed so many lives to be destroyed while Doom's Seed made his money. My teeth gritted.

"Do you know any of the other doctors who were involved?" Beckett asked.

Dr. Evancho shook his head. "I have no idea who else those people brought on. They kept every part of their system totally separate so that there wasn't much chance of any of us turning on them." He looked down at his hands. "That's why I'm not sure I can do anything for you. I hardly know anything."

Dexter glanced at us with a grimace. He was the best at reading people for lies, and he obviously believed this man was telling the truth—there wasn't anything more we could get out of him.

In terms of what he could tell us with his words, anyway. I stepped ahead of the guys, waiting until the doctor met my gaze again.

"We're trying to take those people down for good. We've already put together a lot of the pieces, but we don't have as much concrete evidence as we need to prove our case where it matters. If you have anything you used back then when you were working for them— real records or other references that we could use to prove the ones that the hospitals have now were faked— that could make a huge difference."

His gaze darted briefly to the side. I was pretty sure he was thinking about something he did have that we could use. But he simply twisted his fingers together, a quiver passing through his stout body. "I'm not sure…"

"This is your chance to make up for the harm you helped carry out," I reminded him. "Even if you never hurt anyone directly, you contributed—you bear some of the responsibility. Don't you want to do *something* to fix that?"

Dr. Evancho exhaled shakily and then lifted his head. A trace of determination had come into his eyes.

"I've been holding on to that guilt for a long time. It's been years since I last did anything for those people, but… I believe I do have the original files that I based my falsified ones on. You could use the originals to prove that some of the other records copied data in patterns that are clearly artificial. You'd have to pull the fake records from a lot of different hospitals to prove the repetition, though."

"That's not a problem," Logan said. "Where are the original records?"

"Let me—let me see if I can dig them up."

"Thank you." Beckett motioned to his men. "You go with him in case he needs any assistance."

He said the last word with a little wryness. Mostly he wanted to make sure the doctor didn't betray us somehow, I was sure. We wouldn't want him slipping off and coming back with a weapon.

The doctor hustled out of the room with Beckett's people at his heels. As their footsteps creaked into the basement, Slade cocked his head.

"Do you think he has something that'll really be that useful? Isn't he screwing himself over if he gives it to us?"

"No," Logan said. "Once we have the records, there'll actually be *less* evidence that he was involved, since they won't be stashed here in his house any longer. He'll probably be glad to get rid of them. I doubt he'd have lifted files that were connected to him originally."

My spirits started to rise. "Then this could be something really good."

Beckett smiled at me. "I think it is. And you helped convince him to go along with us. You've been fantastic, Maddie."

Logan brushed his hand over my hair. "She always is."

I wished I could take more enjoyment from their compliments, but all my emotions were tangled up in anticipation. What if Dr. Evancho hadn't held on to the originals after all? What if they'd been damaged beyond use over time?

We waited in silence while thumps and rustling emanated from the floor below. Finally, the doctor and his guards marched back up the stairs and returned to the living room. Dr. Evancho was clutching a manila folder.

He held it out to me. "These are the base files I used for the forgery. They're each from a different hospital—each from a different state. I was trying to be careful."

I flipped open the folder and held it so the guys could scan the papers inside too. They were clearly photocopies, the signatures a little grainy, all from the 1980s.

Dexter got out his phone and snapped pictures of every page so we had a digital copy as well. I glanced at Logan in question after we'd skimmed over the last one, and he gave me a tight smile.

"I can pull it all together. This is everything we need."

I turned back to the doctor. "Thank you. You have no idea how much I appreciate this."

He dipped his head, his expression abruptly softening. "I'm sorry about your father," he said quietly. "I can only imagine he'd have been very proud of you."

A twinge of loss ran through my gut. I swallowed thickly. "I hope so."

In that moment, I could see that for all his waffling and hesitation, Dr. Evancho regretted being a party to this criminal enterprise.

One of Beckett's men pulled himself a little straighter, looming over the doctor, and shot Beckett a pointed look. "Should we do anything else to take care of him?" he asked.

A shiver passed down my spine. I could guess at the implications of that question.

"He knows he's safer from the real villains if he keeps quiet about what he gave us and that we were here," I said to Beckett. "I don't think we need to worry."

And I didn't want to see any more pain coming out of this situation.

Beckett studied me and then the doctor. Dr. Evancho drew up his chin, but it quivered a little.

"My lips are sealed," he insisted. "It'd be a hell of a lot worse for me than for you if those people ever found out. And… I hope you do manage to take them down. I'd like to see that—to know that it's over."

"All right," Beckett said. "Keep an eye on the news, and maybe you will get to see it. I'll remember this." He held up the manila folder.

As we strode out of the house, the tension that'd

gripped me rippled out with a rush of breath. A tingle of excitement took its place. Looking at the folder gripped in Beckett's hand, I couldn't help grinning.

We'd done it. We'd gotten the proof we needed. And those records were going to change *everything*.

CHAPTER
SEVENTEEN

Madelyn

I should have expected nothing less than my mom making the condo her own in three days. When I dropped by and found her in the kitchen, the place held the familiar childhood scent of sautéing garlic and onions. She was making one of her trademark stir-fries.

"I can see you're hanging in there all right," I said lightly.

I could tell Mom's stoic expression was a bit of a front, but she smiled warmly enough that I knew she really was doing okay.

"It's like a little vacation," she said with a laugh. "But I enjoy getting some cooking in. Working with the ingredients is strangely relaxing. And I think Summer is appreciating having a few home-cooked meals. I missed having someone other than Holand to take care of, you know."

"Hey," Holand spoke up from where he was lounging in the living room, peeking over the back of the couch and giving my mom a playful scowl. "I don't need *that* much taking care of."

"Dear, if you could tell the difference between an onion and a potato, I'd be shocked."

I snorted lightly and Holand chuckled, looking back to the television. They seemed like they'd managed to set aside most of the stress that must have been weighing on them after their hasty arrival here and the destruction of the house.

Mom had already started the wheels turning for the insurance. She and Holand had packed their most precious items to keep them close and brought them here anyway, so it hadn't been quite as big of a blow as if the fire had started while they'd been at work… or asleep and unaware.

I updated her on the assignments I'd been squeezing in around the adventures I'd rather not tell her about, and she described the movie they'd all watched last night, but her gaze kept twitching to me as she added chicken and then veggies to the frying pan.

Finally, she sighed and leaned against the counter with her gaze fixed on me. "I have to admit, I keep thinking about your father and how he was mixed up in these criminal enterprises. Do you have any idea how that happened? Or how far this conspiracy you've stumbled on reaches?"

My stomach twisted, but I didn't want to lie to her any more, not unless I absolutely had to. And she deserved to know the full extent of the danger.

"We're pretty sure he came across a medical record from one of the patients who received an illegal transplant and noticed discrepancies in the data," I said. "Somehow he pieced together enough to start tracking down more information at the source. And—it's a big source. Really, really big. We know for sure now that this business extends across multiple states. It could even involve other countries as well."

Mom's jaw tightened. "And you really can't turn to the police and let them handle it?"

"We'd like to. We've been trying to build up enough of a case so that they'll believe there *is* a crime." I let out my breath in a rush. "I think we're almost there. In just a couple more days, you might be able to leave here."

She shook her head, with a distant expression. "I wish your father had never gotten caught up in this mess. Then *you* wouldn't have either."

I swallowed thickly. "That's true, but he was trying to be a hero. He *would* have been a hero if he'd gotten far enough. I'm carrying out the work he wanted to do… just in a different way from what I always pictured. I kind of like that."

"I understand." Mom reached over to squeeze my hand. "But I still don't like the idea of you being involved in something so dangerous. It's *my* job to keep you safe."

I shot her a bittersweet smile. "Not anymore. I'm grown up now—that's my responsibility."

She let out a huff. "I just don't want to see the same thing happen to you that did to him."

"It won't," I said firmly, for both her benefit and my own. "It's different for me. He was trying to go it alone, but I have a bunch of other people standing with me."

No way did I want to admit to her how nervous I actually was, how my nerves shivered just remembering the gunfight at the entertainment complex two evenings ago. That would only make her worry more, and she had enough trauma hanging over her head because of me as it was.

Holand switched off the TV and ambled over to the kitchen to prop himself in the doorway. "Some of those people being Logan and his friends, obviously," he said, and paused. "How is he?"

The strain in his voice and the melancholy shadow that crossed his face brought a fresh lump of guilt into my gut. Logan hadn't come back to the condo since we'd first dropped everyone off here. I knew he still hadn't talked to his dad about Yvonne.

His dad had to be able to tell Logan was keeping things from him. I couldn't imagine how much that would be eating at him with all the things Holand *did* know about his son's activities now.

But it wasn't my place to reveal anything Logan wasn't ready to get into yet.

"He's doing well, all things considered," I said, which seemed both accurate and vague enough.

"I gather that he's been investigating this conspiracy for quite a bit longer than you have. Trying to figure out what happened. He never mentioned anything about it to me at the time."

My voice softened. "I know. He kept me totally in the dark too."

Holand pinched the bridge of his nose. "I wish he would turn to me more. I've tried to be here for him as much as I can."

I didn't know what to tell him, but all of me ached to give him some kind of reassurance.

"He's put a lot of distance between himself and, well, everyone because he's been trying to protect everyone he cares about from the fallout," I said. "Once the mastermind behind all this is arrested and we can breathe easier, I'm sure he'll open up more."

At least, looking into Holand's anguished eyes, I hoped he would. Ultimately, that would come down to Logan and what he felt comfortable with. He'd built a huge wall between him and his dad, and it was hard to say if he'd ever be able to tear it completely down.

Holand gave me a sad but genuine smile. "I'm glad he's been able to turn to you now, at least a little, along with the guys."

"Yeah." I hesitated, and decided that this was one subject I had just as much right to broach as Logan would have. "We've gotten pretty close, you know. Even before you and Mom started dating, there was something between us… I'm looking out for him as well as I can. He means an awful lot to me."

I hadn't been sure if Holand would be able to read between the lines, but a hint of fond amusement sparked in his eyes. "You know, I did wonder back then, watching the two of you together… It's not as if you were ever really raised as siblings."

Mom tsked her tongue behind me and gave my shoulder a squeeze. "As long as you two are being careful in *every* way… I suppose it's good you have each other. We're not going to get in the way of that."

I exhaled slowly, relief sweeping through me. I hadn't really expected them to get uptight about our relationship, but there'd always been a nagging worry in the back of my head. We weren't actually doing anything wrong, though. Holand had never officially adopted me or Mom Logan, so we weren't siblings even in a legal sense.

"I'll give Logan a nudge about coming by to visit," I told Holand. "He's just been so wrapped up in tracing information we've found as well as keeping up with his schoolwork, but soon he won't have the first excuse. Now I'd better go visit the other resident before she accuses me of abandoning her."

"I heard that!" Summer hollered teasingly from her bedroom. "I was just generously giving you some family time before I dragged my bestie away."

"Dinner should be ready in about ten minutes," Mom called after me. "As soon as the rice is done."

I found Summer flopped on her bed, but she sat up

as soon as I came in and patted the mattress for me to join her. Glancing at the huge window that filled one wall of the bedroom, only partly obscured by the sheer curtain hanging over it, she grinned. "You know, this place sure beats my dorm room. I could totally get used to this."

I laughed. "I wouldn't have put you up in a dump. Well, not unless I really had to."

She arched her eyebrows at me. "The friend who owns the place—that's this Beckett of yours, isn't it? He has very good taste in real estate. When do I get to meet him? And does he have any single brothers?"

I couldn't restrain a snort of amusement. "As far as I know, he's an only child. But if I find out otherwise, you'll be the first one I tell."

"Fine." She tipped back over on the bed dramatically and twisted a strand of her hair around her finger. "So what other news have you got? Something must have happened in the past few days."

"Well, we finally got our hands on some evidence that could turn the whole case around," I told her. "We're just making sure we have all our bases covered before we turn it in."

Summer let out a whistle. "Seriously? That's awesome! Then I can stop having panic attacks every time my phone rings, thinking you've been shot or something."

"I'd like that too," I said dryly. "Hopefully we'll have the details settled soon. How's school going with the distance?"

She let out a huff. "One of my professors is being an ass about me taking emergency leave. It doesn't help that I can't explain it. She's a friend of my mom's and I *know* my mom told her that I was lying."

I gasped. "No way."

"You remember how my mom is." Summer groaned. "She loves to know everything, and if she doesn't, she has to act like she does for appearances."

That *was* her mother. I winced. "I don't know how you handle that."

"I don't. There's a reason I never go and see my mom, and that's it."

"So is your professor letting you do the work, or is she refusing?"

"She's letting me do it for appearance's sake, I think. If I took it to the dean that she was giving my mom information on me, she'd be fired in a heartbeat, and she knows it." Summer rolled her eyes. "I can play the game, too."

"I have no idea how my professors are going to take it if I don't end up coming back to classes next week," I admitted. "Another reason I'm grateful it seems like we've almost got this thing wrapped up. I'd love to let the cops handle the rest."

Summer waved a finger at me. "And you *should* let them handle it."

I swatted her. "I know. I just—"

The chime of my phone cut me off. I dug it out of my pocket. As soon as I saw Beckett's name on the screen, I yanked it to my ear.

"What's up?" I asked, and mouthed *Beckett* at Summer. He'd known I was coming to visit Mom and Summer—he wouldn't be interrupting that if it wasn't important.

"Are you still at the condo?" he asked in an urgent tone that set me twice as much on edge.

My heart thumped faster. "I'm sitting beside Summer right now. What happened?"

He took a deep breath, but he couldn't quite erase the raggedness from his voice that showed how unnerved he was. "Have you heard anything there? Has anything happened in or around the building to make you concerned?"

I got up and stepped to the window, but nothing in the view below told me what he might be concerned about. "No, nothing. It's been quiet. No alarms or anything."

"Okay. Okay, good." I caught the thrum of a motor in the background on his end of the line. "I'm on my way to pick you up. Something's gone down—I want you back with me right away. I'm calling in more people to keep watch over the condo building, so everyone there should be safe too. Head down to the lobby now. I'll be there in five minutes."

He hung up abruptly, leaving my nerves on edge. I glanced at Summer, who looked back at me wide-eyed.

"I've got to go," I told her. "Sorry to cut the visit short, but it sounds like there's trouble."

"You go be with your guys," she told me, sitting up

to grab me in a quick hug. "But call me when you can to fill me in."

"Of course."

I hustled out to the kitchen, made hasty apologies to Mom and Holand for missing dinner after all, and squeezed Mom tight before heading out.

The elevator whirred down the building painfully slow. By the time I was crossing the lobby, I spotted Beckett's usual sedan through the glass doors.

The second I came into view, he pushed open the passenger-side door of the car for me. I hopped in and yanked it shut, and he hit the gas before I'd even put on my seatbelt.

"What's going on?" I asked, taking in his tense expression. My heart lurched with panic. "Are the guys—?"

"The other guys are fine," Beckett said quickly. "But only because they haven't left my house since this morning. I—" He shook his head with a slight slump of his shoulders that my heart ached to see.

"What?" I murmured. "What happened?"

His jaw worked. When we had to stop at a red light, he glanced over at me, his normally cool grey eyes stormy with turmoil.

"Doom's Seed has sent his people on a total rampage. They're shooting anyone they can connect to my family's businesses on sight, no matter where they are at the time. Just picking them off in the middle of the street, in regular stores…"

My throat constricted. "Oh my God."

He dipped his head as he urged the car forward again. "It's a bold move, but it's working for him. I've lost over a dozen people in just the last few hours, and if I can't figure out how to end this soon, I'm going to lose even more."

CHAPTER
EIGHTEEN

Slade

Thin sunlight seeped past the curtains on the guestroom window. I groaned and rolled over to bury my head in the pillow, but I already knew it was no use.

Normally I could have tuned out full daylight—not to mention blaring music, animated voices, and anything else going on around me—if I was tired enough. But the turmoil of the past several days had left my nerves on edge. I could barely relax even in total darkness and quiet.

I grimaced, wondering how much actual sleep I'd managed to get between bouts of tossing and turning. From the muggy feeling in my head, I doubted it'd been more than a few hours.

Oh well. I definitely wasn't getting any more now. Might as well chug some coffee and try to make the best of the day, whatever new horrors it might bring.

It was still early, only a little past sunrise. The house was still and silent around me as I swapped the boxers I'd slept in for fresh ones and a tee and sweats combo in case I decided to do a stint in the workout room Beckett had showed us, with an offer of full access. A little exercise might jolt me back into proper alertness.

But first, caffeine.

I padded down the hall and slipped into the sitting room, expecting to find it empty and not wanting to disturb any of the others who would still be sleeping. Just inside the room, I jarred to a halt.

Logan was sitting in the exact same armchair where he'd stationed himself last night, in the exact same clothes, with his laptop poised in front of him. Bags were starting to form under his weary eyes, and his mouth was set in a grim but tired line. Even his short hair looked like it was drooping.

He glanced up at me, his reaction time slowed to a zombie's pace, his gaze hazy as if it took him a few seconds to recognize me.

"Dude, what are you doing awake?" I demanded in a hushed voice, striding over.

"What are *you* doing awake?" he shot back without much vigor.

I eyed him, the wheels in my head turning with suspicion. "Did you even go to bed last night?"

He swiped his hand over his face and appeared to

suppress a yawn. "I had to keep following the trail. Beckett's people farther out have gotten me access to all the hospitals where Dr. Evancho got his base records. I managed to confirm they're all in the system still."

I couldn't help perking up a little even though concern still gripped my gut. "Even though they're from back in the '80s?"

"A lot of older records get digitized over time, especially in fields where quick access could mean life or death. It's a good thing, because we can't be sure even the photocopies would have convinced the cops. Now we can cross-reference to the actual files right in the hospital databases."

"That's great," I had to admit.

Logan nodded in a sluggish motion. "Having the extra data has let me turn up a bunch of other transplant records from all the hospitals we have access to now that are suspect. I think Doom's Seed must have had a few different doctors helping with the forgeries, because there are some repetitions that aren't in any of Evancho's files, but it's still a huge step toward proving our case."

"We're almost there." I glanced from the screen to him again, taking in all the signs of exhaustion etched in his face and his posture. "You didn't answer me before."

"About what?" Logan said in a way that told me he knew exactly what I meant and was only dodging. We hadn't been best friends for years for nothing.

"Did you sleep last night?" I pressed.

He continued looking at his screen, but his eyes stopped moving for a moment, dropping to his keyboard before rising again. "I don't see why it matters."

I narrowed my eyes at him. "You need a break, Logan. This whole case isn't on your shoulders alone."

He sighed and tipped his head against the back of the chair. "There's too much that needs to be done. I need to pull these last pieces together so we can end this before someone else gets hurt. Beckett managed to call all his people to safety last night, but they can't lay low forever. They have lives. Some of them have partners, kids... And now they can't go anywhere without worrying about being shot."

The anguish running through his voice made my stomach knot. Logan put on a solid front of being impervious, but I knew that a lot of things got to him more than he typically let show. And the last few days in particular had been brutal.

"Like I said, it's not all on you." I extended my hand toward the computer. "Tell me what to type in for the searches, and I'll pull some more files while you crash. This isn't worth losing your sanity over. You can't help anyone if you burn yourself out."

Logan groaned. "If I teach you what to do, we'll only be losing more time." He closed his eyes for a few seconds, and his voice dropped even lower. "This whole situation has gotten so much more intense than I was ready for. Maddie's lost her house—our family is in hiding… It's like my worst nightmare coming true. The last thing I want to do is *sleep*."

What the hell could I say to him that would be any comfort? I knew exactly what he meant, even if it didn't hit me quite as hard because it wasn't my family or a house I'd actually lived in.

I rested my hand on his shoulder with a firm grip. "All of that is true. I'm not going to deny it. But Maddie decided to be a part of this as much as you did. Neither of you made these decisions without thinking them through. She has a right to take those risks if she wants to."

"It's my fucking fault for starting all of this in the first place. I have to end it."

I let out a soft snort. "If we're getting technical, it was Maddie's dad who got all of us wrapped up in this case to begin with. If he hadn't poked his nose into it, we'd never have realized. So if you want to blame someone, you might as well blame him, not yourself."

"I insisted on digging into it more instead of just letting it lie," Logan grumbled.

"And if you hadn't, Maddie would never have gotten closure. She'd have kept blaming herself for her dad's death, and more people would have died from this illegal organ transplant shit."

"But at least I wouldn't have to worry about someone gunning her down."

I squeezed his shoulder again. "You know she wouldn't have been any safer if you'd kept it from her. She wouldn't have known she needed to be wary or protect herself. Hell, for all we know, Doom's Seed would have gone after her no matter what we did as soon as he realized she was going into the same field as her father."

Logan let out a sigh, but I heard resigned acceptance in it now. "Everything has become such a clusterfuck."

"Yeah, but we're going to unfuck it." I gave him a crooked grin. "*You* are. I've seen time and time again how hard you work to make things okay for everyone around you. That crazy dedication is part of the reason we're best friends. But it also sometimes works against you. You can't be at your best, giving this your all, when you're running on fumes. It's my job as your friend to tell you when I can see you've hit your limit."

"Yeah," Logan muttered, but he sat straighter to close his laptop and set it on the coffee table. Then he glanced up at me.

"I appreciate the kick in the butt, you know, even when I'm grumbling about it. I know you've always got my back. I have no idea how I'd have made it through the last couple of months—hell, the last couple of *years* —without you and Dex at my side. But you in particular… No matter where my temper's at, highs and lows, you're always there to balance it out and help me get my head on straight."

My smile softened. "Right back at you. And hey, I'm pretty sure my main job around here is cheerleader. I take my duty seriously."

Logan rolled his eyes. "You're a lot more than that. Don't sell yourself short." He paused, his gaze drifting toward the door that led to the hall. "I appreciate that you're here for Maddie too, you know."

My chest tightened just for a second. It wasn't a secret that Logan had struggled with the idea of sharing her affections at first—he'd said some pretty awful things to me a couple of times out of obvious jealousy. But I hadn't let his harsh comments faze me, since I'd known the place they were coming from, and we'd seemed to find an arrangement we were all satisfied with.

I hadn't expected him to outright say he was happy with the situation, though.

"You never have to thank me for loving her," I said lightly. "It's awfully hard not to."

"I just mean…" He shook his head. "It was stupid of me to go all caveman, thinking I should have her to myself. More and more, I can see how we all offer her different things, make her life better in different ways, and that's really pretty amazing."

He stopped, his jaw working, and then added, "I don't think I'm in the right headspace to give her what she needs right now. She's got to be stressed out too, and I can tell I'd only amplify that. But…" He caught my gaze again. "Maybe you could help her work through the shit she's grappling with like you have for me."

The words felt almost like a command—or maybe that wasn't generous enough of me. An invitation, a gesture of mutual respect, making it totally clear that he not only accepted my role in Maddie's life but welcomed it. Encouraged it, even.

A warmth filled my chest, the brotherly love I held for the man next to me and the sweeter adoration for the woman we both cared about so much mingling together.

"I'll see what I can do," I said, and gave Logan a gentle shove. "Leave it to me, and try not to worry about that too. Dr. Slade orders you to get at least three hours of sleep before you open up that computer again. I don't think that's asking too much."

Logan muttered something inarticulate, but there was gratitude in his last glance before he hauled himself out of the chair and headed back to his own guest room.

My own restlessness had settled down after our conversation, seeing that I'd made a difference with him, knowing how confident he was in my ability to help both him and Maddie through the mess we'd found ourselves in. Why shouldn't I find out if I could work a little of that spirit-lifting magic on her right now? If she was still sleeping, I didn't think she'd mind starting with a snuggle.

My own spirits buoyed, I set off down the hall myself. I was still several steps from Maddie's guestroom door when it opened.

Maddie stepped out, rubbing her eyes, looking perfectly gorgeous even dressed in casual leggings and a loose tee with her pale hair sleep-rumpled. She shot me a tired-looking smile.

"Trouble sleeping?" I asked, ambling over to her.

"Yeah." She looked me over. "I'm guessing that's going around?"

"It seems to be." As I stood there in front of her, basking in her presence, inspiration sparked in my head. "Might as well make the most of it. Come out for breakfast with me?"

"*Out* for breakfast?" Maddie repeated, cocking her head in surprise.

I reached out to her. "You'll see."

She took my hand without hesitation, and I knew I'd better make the most of the opportunity while I had it.

CHAPTER
NINETEEN

Madelyn

When I met Slade at the back door of the mansion after a quick change, I couldn't help raising my eyebrows. His hoodie and sweats combo wasn't particularly unusual, but his shoes…

"You know," I said, "I think this is the first time I've ever seen you in sneakers that aren't the flashiest possible color."

Slade looked down at the black shoes he was wearing and chuckled. "I had to borrow these from Logan. Good thing he's only one size bigger than my usual. I figured there wasn't much point in trying to be covert if my sneakers were acting like a neon sign." He slung his arm around my shoulders. "Come on."

"Are you sure this is a good idea?" I murmured as we slipped out into the backyard that seemed to stretch an entire city block, expanses of grass and beds of flowers broken by the occasional stately tree. I tugged my hood a little higher over my hair.

By the time we'd turned in for the night, Beckett had managed to contact all of his people who lived or worked anywhere near Doom's Seed's territory and make sure they were staying out of the public eye and keeping their homes secure. We didn't know if the previous attackers were still patrolling the city looking for targets, but if they happened to spot us, I doubted they'd hesitate to take aim.

"We can get away for a little bit and still stay safe." Slade leaned over to give me a quick peck to the side of my head. "I scoped out exit routes from the mansion a couple of days ago. There's a spot where we can leave without anyone being the wiser, even if Doom's Seed has eyes on the house."

A nervous quiver ran through my pulse, but there was a little excitement in it too. That was why I hadn't turned Slade down when he'd explained this part of his plan.

It felt good to be defying our enemy's reign of terror, to prove that he couldn't completely control us. And right now, proving that might be the only thing keeping me from being overwhelmed by a sense of hopelessness.

There wasn't anything else Slade or I could do to help solidify the final pieces of evidence for the cops now. And when was the last time I'd really let myself simply breathe and enjoy a moment for myself?

"Here we go," Slade said under his breath as we reached the stone wall that surrounded the property, a little taller than I was. He tipped his head to one of Beckett's men who was patrolling nearby, and the guy nodded back without a hint of concern.

It figured that Slade had already made friends with the guards.

A bench stood under a tree a few feet from the wall. Slade grabbed it and dragged it over before clambering onto it. Then he motioned for me to join him. "We're going up and over."

I climbed after him and peeked over the top of the wall. Another yard lay beyond it.

"Are you sure we won't get arrested for trespassing?"

"Not if we're quick about it. Come on, Piccolina. This isn't even close to the most dangerous thing we've done in the past week."

I glowered at him, but my mouth twitched with a smile at the same time. "Fine." He was making this an adventure, maybe specifically to distract me from the much more frightening adventure we were already wrapped up in, and I couldn't say I minded that.

He lowered his hands to give me a boost, and I set my foot on his palm. At his heft, I scrambled over the top of the wall and landed with a thump on the other side.

Slade heaved himself after me with just a faint thunk when his prosthetic bumped the edge of one of the stones. He dropped down with a grin already in place. "Almost there."

To my relief, we veered straight across the lawn to a hedge that ran along one side of the yard and pushed through a gap between the bushes onto a narrow but apparently public laneway. No one shouted out anything about trespassers, so we were home free.

Slade took my hand and tugged me along to the end of the lane. He peered out into the quiet street on the other side, checking for suspicious activity. Then we jogged across the road and into a sprawling park I hadn't realized was here.

A line of trees stood along this edge of the park, and in less than a minute, I could no longer see the street behind us. My shoulders came down, my nerves soothed by the knowledge that no one would spot us unless they specifically came looking for us here. And there was no way Doom's Seed could guess we'd have taken this little side-trip.

"You planned a breakfast picnic in the park?" I asked, still keeping my voice low, although it might not have been necessary. This early in the morning, the park was empty other than a lone jogger who puffed past us on one of the paths.

"This is a step up even from that. You'll see."

Slade urged me around another glade of trees, and then I stopped in my tracks, gaping at the structure in front of us.

A large, old-fashioned carousel stood in the middle of the clearing next to the path. Beneath its peaked roof, an assortment of wooden horses gamboled and reared, a few drawing chariots and sleighs, most of them with saddles that had posts through the pommels. The paint was worn, but I could tell from the faded remains that it'd once been vibrant. Here and there, spots shone with gold detailing.

"Wow," I said, collecting my jaw. "What kind of city park has one of these just sitting here?"

Slade laughed. "The kind of park you'd find in a neighborhood for people this rich, I guess. How's that for a picnic spot?"

I beamed at him. "Perfect. But where's the breakfast?"

"All in good time, Piccolina. Why don't you pick your seat?"

I circled the carousel until I spotted a sleigh that looked large enough to allow us to sit next to each other without getting too cramped. As I settled into the seat, Slade glanced toward the path. He waved to someone and then loped over to meet a skinny man in a windbreaker who'd just emerged from the shelter of the trees, carrying a couple of paper delivery bags.

Slade took the bags from the man with a bright smile and a thank you and carried them back to the sleigh. "Breakfast is served! I had someone from one of those food apps pick it up from a café in the neighborhood so we didn't have to be seen out there."

I shook my head at him, but affection tingled through me at how much forethought he'd put into this plan. He'd made what could have been a simple breakfast date into something almost magical amid all the chaos we were facing.

I couldn't imagine any of the other guys being able to pull that off.

Slade tucked himself in next to me on the seat, propping one foot against the opposite bench, and retrieved the items from the bags with a flourish. "Coffee, yours with plenty of cream and some cinnamon along with the sugar. Breakfast sandwiches in croissants. Fresh cut fruit, and custard pastries for dessert."

The savory and sweet smells flooded my nose, making my mouth water. "This looks amazing," I said, taking in the spread he'd laid out on the narrow table between the seats.

"Here's hoping it tastes at least half as good," Slade said with a twinkle in his eye.

I leaned over to claim a swift kiss. "I'm sure it does. Thank you."

His expression softened, and he touched my cheek. "You deserve this. We haven't had much chance to spoil you—much chance to do anything except make sure no one's shooting you down, in a while. This is what our life should look like. What it will look like, when we've gotten through this rough patch. I wanted to give you a preview so you know what you have to look forward to."

I hadn't known my heart could swell with any more love than it already had, but right then, I felt close to bursting. I twined my fingers with his and squeezed them tightly before turning back to our food. "We'd better dig in while the sandwiches are still warm. I'm starving."

Slade unwrapped one sandwich and handed it to me, his fingers brushing mine, his shoulder resting companionably against me. When the buttery croissant melted on my tongue, mingling with the creaminess of the egg and cheese within and the tartness of the sliced tomato, I almost swooned. He'd chosen well.

"This is delicious," I told him, snuggling a little closer. "You get full points."

His eyes sparkled. "The only win I need is having you here with me."

We both made short work of our sandwiches and then discovered that the sliced fruit was all in the same container. Slade jabbed the plastic fork into a chunk of pineapple and held it toward me. "Allow me."

I gave him a playfully baleful look but opened my mouth. When he popped the fruit between my lips, the sweet-and-sour juice had my taste buds singing.

"My turn," I said, snatching the fork from him, and raised a slice of orange to his lips.

We devoured the entire container of fruit that way, going back and forth. More and more heat collected low in my belly with each glimpse of some tidbit disappearing into Slade's skilled mouth. When he licked his lips after the last morsel, a quiver shot straight to my pussy. For a second, I forgot that the point was to eat.

Slade hadn't. He retrieved the custard pastries from the second bag and offered one to me.

The custard flooded my mouth, the perfect mix of smooth and creamy, and I couldn't hold back a groan. Slade's gaze lingered on my face as I polished off the pastry in record time. Then he leaned toward me.

"You missed a little."

He dabbed his thumb at the corner of my mouth to wipe a little blob of custard and then held it out for me. Meeting his eyes, I sucked the tip of his thumb into my mouth. It was hard to say what I enjoyed more—the last bit of sweetness or the flare of desire in his dark gaze.

"And now I need to return the favor," he said, his voice getting husky, and caught my hand in his. He brought my fingers to his mouth and flicked out his tongue to lick the crumbs off each tip, one after the other. With each gentle but heated swipe, I could feel my panties dampening.

By the time he reached my little finger, I was holding myself back from squirming in my seat. My thighs pressed together against the ache between my legs.

But Slade had never been one to leave me hanging. He slid his fingers up my arm to my shoulder and then down my side before tugging me onto his lap. "I don't think I've quite had my fill yet."

His mouth descended on mine, the delectable flavors of the meal mingling together with the heat of desire that'd already kindled between us. I arched into the kiss, and his arms wrapped around me, holding me tight.

Slade's lips melded with mine, coaxing them open so his tongue could slip between them and tease over my own. He tilted his head to deepen the kiss, one hand stroking up and down my torso. His fingers caught on the hem of my hoodie and slipped beneath it to stroke the bare skin of my waist where my T-shirt had ridden up.

A whimper traveled up my throat. I wanted more, so much more of this gorgeous, playful, and devoted man who'd created one of the most romantic moments of my life in the middle of a maelstrom.

His fingers crept up my side toward my breasts and brushed over the cups of my bra. Another needy sound tumbled out of me, but when I opened my eyes to gaze into Slade's, my awareness of the world around us snapped back into sharper focus.

We were still sitting in the carousel sleigh, the wider park all around us. No one had come by so far, but that didn't mean they wouldn't.

I hesitated automatically, and Slade eased back a bit to study my expression. "Everything all right?"

I bit my lip. "Anyone could come by and see us. Maybe we should take this back to the house."

Slade let out a low chuckle and nuzzled my neck just below my ear, a spot that sent a giddy tingle rushing over my skin. "I'd have thought that was a benefit, not a problem, considering how we got started. You seem to enjoy a little risk. But I guess we did have a little more cover in the library. Let's see if I can find the right balance for you, Piccolina."

Without warning, he lifted me into the air and tucked me against his chest as he strode around the carousel. "Slade!" I protested half-heartedly.

"Hmm," he said, ignoring my chiding. "This should put us out of view from the path."

He set me down on one of the wooden horses that was poised on its pole close to the carousel floor. With me perched sideways on its saddle, facing Slade, I was just the right height for him to step between my splayed knees.

He tangled his fingers in my hair and dipped his head close to mine. "No one should notice us here unless they go out of their way to peek, in which case it's their fault—or if you make too much noise, in which case it's yours."

I trembled eagerly at the wicked amusement in his voice and couldn't resist tugging him to me for another kiss.

As our mouths collided again and again, I rocked against Slade's waist. He teased his fingers over my chest, delving right inside my bra to roll my nipples until I gasped. Swallowing the sound, he stroked me again and again until I was clutching at him, my lips searing against his with my desire to connect with him in every possible way.

Then his hand skimmed down my body to my sweatpants. He hooked his fingers around the waistband and hefted me up an inch with his other hand, managing to tug the fabric right off me. I only realized he'd taken my panties with them when he set me back down and I felt my bare ass against the aged wood.

"You taste so good, Maddie," he murmured. "But there's more of you I want to taste before we're through."

"Slade," I mumbled, picking up on his intention before he'd even sunk to his knees.

He leaned between my thighs and flicked his thumb over my clit and lower. "So wet for me already. That's my girl."

At my whimper, he pressed his mouth up against me. His tongue swept over and then into my slit, parting me with a bolt of pure bliss. His upper lip worked against my clit, massaging pulses of pleasure into it as his tongue consumed me.

I tried to hold back any louder sounds, but my breath broke into pants despite my best efforts. "Please," I gasped. "Please."

All at once, his tongue swiped upward to swivel around my clit. Two fingers plunged into me, curling to press against the neediest spot inside me. With just a few enthusiastic deep thrusts, sucking me down at the same time, I was shattering apart.

As the rush of pleasure crashed over me, I shuddered against his mouth. Slade hummed approvingly, the sound reverberating into my body, and kissed me there again.

Then he was moving up my body, his fingers keeping up their steady pumping rhythm inside me, his mouth branding my belly, my ribs, my sternum, my breast. As he let my shirt fall again, he captured my lips.

The faint taste of myself on him made me shiver. He paused in his fondling to grip my thigh in balance as he fumbled in his pocket with his other hand. The second he'd torn open the packet with his teeth and slicked the contents over himself, he caught me in his embrace again.

His fingers returned to my pussy, and his lips claimed all the whimpers and moans that I couldn't hold back. He teased me until I was jerking my hips into his talented hand, and then he swapped it in an instant to thrust the entire, hard length of his cock into me.

I almost sobbed with the pleasure of it filling me. My legs tightened around his hips. Slade gave a soft groan and gripped my ass so he could slam into me even harder.

The fresh, cool morning breeze wove around us, tickling against my bare legs and rustling through the leaves of the nearby trees. I barely noticed our surroundings though, lost in the flood of bliss this man was conjuring in my body.

He pounded into me over and over, only his grasp keeping me from tumbling off my wooden mount in our passion. Our mouths pressed together wildly, our breaths shaking.

"Oh, Piccolina," Slade muttered in between kisses. "You're perfect. Only you've ever made me feel this good. I want all your sounds, all your sweetness."

Another gasp broke from my lips, and he thrust into me even faster. The force sent me spinning into ecstasy.

My orgasm blazed through me. Stars sparked behind my eyes. In that moment, it was only me and Slade in the whole world as he grunted out a choked sound with his own release.

We clung together for a minute, sweat-damp and sated. Slade brushed the hair back from my forehead and kissed me there, then my nose, then my mouth again.

"My girl and our girl," he said softly. "I'll always find a way to win that smile, no matter what else is going on around us."

An ache filled my heart, but I believed him.

I hugged him tightly until reality sank in a little too much. When I hopped down from the horse, he helped me reassemble my clothes and tugged his own pants up. A blush colored my cheeks as we gathered the remains of our breakfast, as if someone would appear now and accuse us of public indecency.

But no one crossed our path until we were heading back through the park, having tossed the garbage in one of the public bins, and the woman walking her terrier didn't give us a second glance. I leaned against Slade, our hands entwined, adrift on a sense of peace.

It didn't last long, though. The moment we reached the road, needing to scan it carefully before crossing to the secluded ally, my worries started to creep back in again.

We pushed through the hedge and heaved ourselves

over the stone wall without incident. With every step, though, I pushed myself a little faster.

What if something new had gone wrong while we were away? What if another catastrophe was just waiting to crash down on our heads?

Slade squeezed my hand. "It's going to be okay, Maddie. Whatever happens, whatever comes, we're going to get through it."

His words reassured me enough that I managed to walk at a less panicked pace up the stairs and down the hall to Beckett's rooms. We stepped inside to find all three of the other guys there, Logan sprawled on the sofa, Dexter perched in the neighboring armchair, and Beckett standing over them both.

Our host lifted an eyebrow at the sight of us. "Where have you two been?"

Slade moved his arm around my waist. "I was just making sure our woman got some much-needed R and R." He paused to glower down at Logan. "Weren't you supposed to be sleeping for at least another hour?"

"I tried," Logan muttered. "The room was too… empty. I might be able to nap in here." He glanced up at me and patted the cushion next to him. "Sit with me?"

How could I refuse him? I sank down onto the sofa and cuddled up to Logan's weary form. He sighed and tipped his head against my shoulder as if he'd been waiting just for me before he could relax.

Dexter pushed himself off his chair and settled onto the floor by my feet, curling his fingers around my calf in a gentle massage. He pressed a kiss to my knee that left my heart fluttering.

Beckett leaned over the back of the couch to caress his fingers over my hair. And Slade grinned at us all as he dropped into the other armchair, as if he'd orchestrated this moment for me too.

I *was* their woman—all of theirs—and I'd never felt it more than in this moment, surrounded by their shared affection.

We were so close to having this happiness without any threats looming over us. Please, let what we'd gotten be enough to see us through to the end.

CHAPTER
TWENTY

Madelyn

"Go through everything again with me," Slade said, holding up a list of all the compiled evidence we had. We'd organized it as well as we could, with an explanatory letter laying out all the connections and highlighting the important aspects, and gathered it both in a packet of printed materials and a flash drive.

Beckett had even set up a scheduled email—one that would send if we didn't return and refresh the settings within two days. The message would go directly to the police department, with all the digital files and a note that something must have happened to all of us related to the case.

It was a precaution, just in case we never made it all the way to the cops to begin with.

Dexter leafed through the packet of hard copies. "We've got the photocopies and printouts of all the relevant hospital records, our notes on the seafood market and the operating facility where it was sending 'poisonous fish' along with key photographs, business records showing what front company owns that business and others, and a statement about the possible drug exchange Madelyn witnessed at the spa. And printouts of my photos of Evan Silver's relevant notes with related documentation."

The original notes and some other concrete evidence had been lost in the fire in the Vigil office at the university, but Dexter's relentless commitment to documentation had filled most of that gap.

I bobbed restlessly on my feet, wanting to think everything was about to fall into place for us but hesitant to get my hopes all the way up. "And all of that is on the flash drive in digital form too?"

Logan nodded. "I double-checked. And it has the video files that we couldn't fully add to the printed packet too."

I let out my breath in a rush. "Okay. It seems like that should be everything. All of this stuff has got to be enough, right?"

The five of us studied the thick folder, packed with all our assembled proof. "I can't say I have a lot of faith in the police," Beckett said. "But I feel like this much evidence has to be enough to get them started on an investigation of their own, even if they can't make any arrests right off the bat. And they have more resources than we do to make even more connections."

Slade tapped his prosthetic foot on the floor. "It'd be better if we had a direct witness. Too bad Dr. Evancho barely wanted to give us as much as he did."

I hugged myself. "If the police don't take action, we can always push harder on him, I guess."

"Or go to the media," Dexter added. "There's some provocative material in here—if they print some stories on the situation, it'll put pressure on the cops to take a look."

"Right." I forced a smile. "I just hope they can arrest Doom's Seed—whatever his real name is—fast. Because he's *really* not going to be happy with us once he figures out we've exposed his businesses to the police."

Logan gripped my shoulder. "We won't let anything happen to you. We've made it this far okay, haven't we?"

"I'm not the only one I'm worried about," I reminded him. "You've all become targets too—and everyone working under Beckett."

"Once the cops are on the case, we'll have some protection from Doom's Seed and his people," Slade said. "He'll know how closely the police will scrutinize the situation if we're even hurt. It might piss him off, but exposing him protects us too."

He had a point. I tried to focus on that rather than my lingering anxiety. "Okay. So we're ready to go?"

"Hold on." Logan dropped onto the sofa and

opened his laptop. "I want to reconfirm one last thing about the source records. Then we're good to go."

As he tapped at the keys to regain access to the hospital networks he'd been patched into, I gave the other guys a crooked smile. "It's going to be weird when this is over. The investigation has been scary, but it's also what brought us all together."

Slade smirked. "I'd like to think we'd have found each other even without the case, Piccolina. Once we crossed paths on campus, you wouldn't have been able to stay away from me."

As the corners of my lips twitched higher at his teasing, Beckett shook his head. "We met before I even knew there was an investigation. Although I'm awfully glad I ended up being here to help you navigate my part of the world."

Logan let out a grunt that had us all glancing toward him. His forehead had furrowed. "That's weird," he muttered.

My pulse hiccupped. "What?"

"I can't get the right files to load. Give me a second."

As Logan's fingers flew across the keyboard, the rest of us gathered behind the sofa to watch. The sense of unease that'd been prickling through my chest grew claws, sinking deeper in.

Logan's keystrokes grew more forceful with each iteration. Then his hands clenched into fists.

"It doesn't make sense. I just looked at the originals in the hospital systems last night. This record was here then, and now it's like it never existed."

"Check a file at one of the other hospitals," Beckett suggested, but the tightening of his face told me he didn't feel any better about this development than I did.

My heart sank as Logan repeated the process on a different server. And then another, and another, and another. His head drooped farther with each failure.

Finally, he sagged back against the sofa cushions. "They're all gone—all of the original records that Dr. Evancho photocopied and drew data from."

I swallowed thickly. "Does it matter? We still have the photocopies."

"Yeah, but without the proof that those are real hospital records themselves, it could look like we made *those* up to try to prove our case. Fuck!"

Slade looked sick. "Someone deleted them from the system?"

"They must have," Logan muttered. "And no prizes for guessing who that someone must have been."

"But—Doom's Seed left them there for so long," I protested. "The whole time we've been investigating. We didn't go anywhere near the hospitals the records came from ourselves—it was all through Beckett's connections. Why would Doom's Seed have suddenly —" My pulse stuttered. "Dr. Evancho. If someone was keeping an eye on him and realized we'd gotten to him…"

Logan was already tapping at the keyboard again. He brought up a list of search results and clicked on the top one. I'd already braced myself before my eyes caught on the text.

It was an obituary, posted just a couple of hours ago. *Dr. Steve Evancho, survived by his son, Jason Evancho, and his wife, Mary Evancho.*

Logan scowled as his gaze darted over the screen. "It claims he died of a heart attack in the middle of the night."

Slade made a scoffing sound. "Unlikely."

"Doom's Seed arranged his death like he did my dad's," I said with a shiver. Only a much faster health crisis. I had no doubt at all that the heart attack hadn't been provoked by natural causes.

Yet another death in the long list that should have been on Doom's Seed's conscience, not that I believed he cared the slightest bit.

"He must have found out the doctor had been compromised somehow," Beckett said in a rough voice. "Now he's launching an even broader cover-up than before."

A sense of hopelessness settled over me that I saw reflected on all of the guys' faces. Logan pushed away his laptop and raked his hand back through his hair.

"Those source records were the cornerstone of our evidence," Dexter said quietly. "Without the originals to prove they're real, they're worthless."

I groped for any possible solution. "The real originals were paper records—the ones Dr. Evancho photocopied. Could those still be at the hospitals?"

"I doubt it," Logan said. "They were almost definitely destroyed after being digitized—that's part of the point of digitization, to free up physical storage space. And if they weren't, what are the chances Doom's Seed *didn't* make sure those vanished too?"

He was right, of course. Slade looked at the floor and then around at the rest of us. "So what do we do now?"

That was the question, wasn't it? We could still try to approach the police, but it felt almost pointless when the veracity of our most key evidence would immediately be called into question.

Beckett's phone rang. He ignored it for a moment, lost in a pensive daze, before he pulled it from his pocket. My stance stiffened even more as he brought it to his ear. We couldn't take any more bad news.

"Beckett here," he said, and then paused. Whatever the person on the other end said, it brought a shadow across Beckett's face, his brow knitting. He sucked in a breath. "Okay. I'll be right there."

He hung up and turned to us. "I have to go. Hopefully it won't take long."

My eyebrows leapt up. "Go? Right now?"

"It's—it could be important. I can't just ignore it. But I'll be back as soon as I can."

With those words hanging in the air, he hurried out of the room.

CHAPTER
TWENTY-ONE

Beckett

I rushed across the house as fast as my feet could carry me without looking outright panicked in front of the guards stationed nearby. The door to my father's home office was closed, but he knew I was coming, so I pushed right inside without knocking.

He was the one who'd summoned me, after all.

I stopped just over the threshold with the door thumping shut behind me. Dad looked up at me from his office chair, his hands folded on top of the desk in front of him.

His face still looked weary, and his hair was more rumpled than he'd have allowed it to get in the old days when he was as strict about his appearance as he'd been about everything else. But there was a firmness to his expression that I hadn't seen in months… maybe years. A renewed alertness in his eyes.

He could almost have passed for the man he'd been before I'd betrayed him to my friends in Paradise Bend.

"What's going on?" I asked, drawing myself up a little straighter instinctively under his scrutiny. He wouldn't have called me in for a face-to-face meeting unless it was important.

If he'd found some of his old spirit, could I dare to hope that we didn't need the intervention of the police at all? That Dad and I could rain down hellfire on Doom's Seed together and obliterate him and his men from this city?

"I realized that we should talk about the current conflict between our forces and Doom's Seed," Dad said, adding fuel to my hopes. "I gather you've been taking the lead on dealing with his people's offensives against us."

My throat tightened. "Yes. I've been giving Lana regular reports to pass on to you, but the ongoing attacks have required so much of my attention—I've been doing my best to handle the situation without needing to interrupt your other work."

I hadn't believed he'd have anything useful to offer was more like it, but I wasn't going to admit that to his face.

Dad nodded. "I appreciate that. It sounds as though you've done a capable job of rising to the occasion, as difficult as it's been. But you've done enough."

My spirits leapt for just an instant before he spoke his next words. "It's time to back down."

Any elation I'd felt snuffed out. I stared at him, my jaw going slack. I had to gather myself before I could speak. "What are you talking about?"

"We're going to cut our losses and pull out of the city," Dad said, coolly and steadily. "Let him have our territory there if he wants it so much. We don't need the handful of businesses we've established there—they're just a drop in the bucket of our holdings. It's not worth continuing the conflict."

My stomach knotted. "Are you kidding me? You want to just lay down and let him steal from us? How's that going to look to the rest of the Devil's Dozen?"

Dad fixed me with an unexpectedly steely glare. "If you're going to really become the Storm one day and stand at the table as their equal, you need to know not every battle is worth fighting."

Was *he* seriously claiming some kind of higher wisdom on that subject? The man who just seven years ago had poured so many resources into a pointless takeover that'd stretched our manpower and resources thin—that we'd only emerged from mostly unscathed because *I'd* stepped in and forced an end to the war?

"I do know that," I said, unable to stop an edge from creeping into my voice. "I also know that ceding established ground to another power is one of the first things you told me we never do. It'll only invite more attacks from other quarters. Maybe we can afford to lose our properties in the city, but how much else are we going to lose next? This house is less than an hour away from the downtown core!"

"And there's no reason for Doom's Seed to be interested in our family home. You may have taken on a lot of responsibility in recent years, but you're not the head of the family yet. I call the shots. And I say that it's become clear that our attempts at holding our local business properties are coming at too high a cost."

I held back a snort of derision. Now of all times he'd decided to start thinking about practicalities, after years of barely paying attention to our profit sheets? The urge to bring up all the investments we'd recently made in the city itched at the base of my throat, but another, chilling thought shot through me before I could speak.

Yes, why *was* he suddenly interested in getting involved?

I narrowed my eyes at him. "Did Doom's Seed contact you—say something to you that made you come to this decision?" We hadn't lost any more people in the latest attack on us since last night, almost twenty-four hours ago. It seemed odd that Dad would be spurred into motion now by that or anything else I knew about.

Dad's mouth flattened. "I can make my own evaluations of our dealings. It's not your place to question me."

"I think it is," I shot back. "I've been the one in charge for the last four years, in all but name. I've been the one handling the day-to-day business and most of the big transactions as well. I've been on the front lines of this battle for weeks, and I have no idea how much you even know what's been going on. So I think I have a right to ask for answers. Did he talk to you or not?"

Dad stood up, slamming his hand against the desktop as he did. "You'll listen to me," he snapped, a hint of a tremor creeping into his words. "I practically lost you once. I'm not letting it happen again."

A stillness swept over me, my chest constricting even more than before. "He did talk to you, didn't he? He threatened *me*? You can't listen to him, Dad. I can look after myself. We have to—"

"We don't have to do anything," Dad cut in. "We're ending this now, with no more bloodshed on either side."

"It's not really you making that call if you're only doing it because he threatened you."

Dad's mouth twisted. "He has the power here. I know how many men we've lost. If he goes ahead and comes right at the home I've worked so hard to build, at you..."

His voice faltered, and his shoulders sagged.

My heart lurched. I stepped toward him. "He called you up and told you that if you didn't back down, he'd attack us right in our home? Kill me? That fucking asshole—"

"It doesn't matter," Dad muttered, all but confirming what I'd said. "I'm not risking it. I took too many gambles in the past, and they could have gone even more badly than they did... I'm not testing my luck again."

Anger flared up inside me. "No. I can't believe you're letting him bully you after everything— This is *my* legacy you're trying to throw away now. Everything I've been working for, everything I've built. It's not just yours anymore. You don't get to decide all of a sudden that you're going to protect me and ruin everything that I've made mine."

And how dare that smug bastard Doom's Seed go behind my back and make his brutal threats to a man he obviously realized no longer had as much backbone as I did.

But Doom's Seed wasn't here for me to aim my anger at, and my father was. Even now, Dad was setting his jaw, ready to fight with me when he should have been fighting our enemy.

"I'm doing this to protect our empire," he insisted.

"Bullshit. When was the last time you even attended one of the Devil's Dozen meetings? They can all smell blood in the water, and I've been able to hold it together —by doing things my way. By showing a strong front. You let this slide, and everything we own is going to fall down like dominos."

Dad shook his head. "I've had enough failures without losing my home and my son too. My decision is final."

"Please, Dad," I said, my voice breaking. "Really think about this. Listen to me."

"I've already done all the thinking I need to."

I dragged in a breath, an ache coiling in my gut. There was no getting through to him, was there? I'd already known that—it was why I hadn't gone to him for advice about the situation in the first place.

The man who'd been the Storm, who'd raised me to follow in his footsteps, had stumbled right off the path he'd always taught me to follow, and there was no way I could yank him back onto it when he'd let his spirit be crushed.

And maybe it was partly my fault that he'd become so diminished, but I couldn't see how it would have been better if I hadn't prevented the full catastrophe that Paradise Bend could have been. So really, he'd destroyed himself.

It was time I stopped blaming myself for that and put the responsibility where it belonged.

He'd had the chance to build our empire, and I wouldn't give him another opportunity to tear it down.

I squared my shoulders. "I'm not giving in, Dad. I've been taking your role as the Storm for years now. I've formed alliances and taken care of all the good, bad, and dirty business while you stayed holed up in here like a recluse. This final decision is mine, not yours. And I'm not giving up."

Dad glared at me, a look that might have shaken my nerves when I'd been a teenager. But I wasn't a kid anymore. I could hold my own now.

His jaw worked, but he could obviously tell I wasn't going to back down. A sigh escaped him.

"You won't get very far if you try to continue the crusade. I've told our local people not to participate any more in the conflict, no matter what you say. You can't take on Doom's Seed alone."

Shit. I hadn't believed he'd go that far. He'd underestimated our people—at this point, some of them would follow me no matter what he said—but others were still more loyal to him than to me. He was leaving me with even less manpower than I'd had after Doom's Seed's attacks.

"Don't do this," I said. "It's a mistake—just as big a mistake as trying to take Paradise Bend was."

Rage flashed across Dad's face. I'd poked an even sorer spot than I'd realized.

"I suppose we'll see who's right in the end, won't we?" he growled.

I'd gotten my stubbornness from him. He assumed I'd have to give in if I didn't have the resources to continue.

And maybe some part of him really did believe he was doing it to save me.

It was no good arguing with him anymore. "I suppose we will," I retorted, spinning on my heel, and stalked out of the room.

As I strode down the hall, my thoughts whirled in my head. I couldn't let Doom's Seed win. I might as well hand over our entire empire to the rest of the Devil's Dozen and whoever they'd appoint as the Storm in my place once they'd picked over the pieces. But how the fuck was I going to stop him when I'd already been struggling with the resources I had?

I couldn't even hope that going to the police would

put an end to the conflict, not when Doom's Seed had undermined our evidence so thoroughly. Even if they took a look at what we did have, I couldn't imagine it'd be sooner than months from now when they might finally dig up enough to even arrest a few of his people.

I was on my own.

That thought stopped me in my tracks. I paused, thinking back over the argument with my dad—and the history at the center of the tension between us.

Seven years ago, I'd run to Paradise Bend when the ruling gangs there were in trouble so that I could help them turn the tide—at my own father's expense. Those gangs had survived because of my help and grown more powerful in the years since. They might not compete on a global scale like the Devil's Dozen members, but a local territory conflict? They were more than equipped for that.

And if I'd ever needed my friends to return the favor I'd done for them all those years ago, now was definitely the time.

CHAPTER
TWENTY-TWO

Madelyn

couldn't help feeling a little nervous as the Vigil guys and I ventured out into the yard behind Beckett's mansion, where dozens of strangers were milling around.

I knew Beckett had plenty of criminal ties from high-level, white-collar types like himself all the way down to minor gangs. But the two crews he'd told us he'd called in were both powerful and yet not at all like him—the two gangs who jointly ruled an entire county called Paradise Bend, which Beckett had told me he'd helped save in defiance of his father years ago.

He'd spent a lot of time with the leaders of these gangs. He considered them his closest friends, and they were clearly ready to do anything for him, given that they'd shown up so quickly and with so many of their people for support. But I couldn't help wondering what they'd make of me and the Vigil guys with our limited experience with the criminal life.

Every man who prowled across the lawn past us looked hardened and dangerous. Several gazes slid over us with expressions that varied from puzzled to incredulous. I hugged myself, fighting the urge to duck back inside.

These were our allies, the people who'd stand with us against Doom's Seed. I couldn't let appearances scare me off now, not when we were hoping to end this war today.

Slade clicked the cinnamon candy he'd popped into his mouth against his teeth. "Whoa. Now this is an army."

Logan frowned. "We just need a target to point them at."

Beckett emerged from the crowd with five figures striding along behind him. He flashed his brilliant smile at us, and a little of the tension inside me melted.

He trusted these people—cared about these people—and *I* trusted his judgment. They might look frighteningly cold and vicious, but I'd seen Beckett bring out his savage side when he needed to too. I knew it didn't stop him or them from having a solid moral compass, one I might agree with a lot more often than not.

"I'd like you to meet my good friends, the leaders of the Claws and the Nobles from Paradise Bend," Beckett said with his smile still in place, and motioned the others to gather around him. "This is Mercy, who keeps the Claws in hand all by herself."

The woman he'd motioned to let out a husky chuckle with a swish of her dark brown ponytail. She was about the same height as me, but her body was sinewy with muscle, and she gave off a similar air of total confidence to what I'd always admired in Beckett.

"I do get a little help here and there," she said with apparent amusement, and dipped her head to us in acknowledgment. "Glad to meet you, but I wish it wasn't because one of these Devil's Dozen pricks is threatening Beckett."

Well, I could agree with that sentiment. I found myself smiling back at her.

Beckett motioned to the four guys next. "This bunch wrangles the Nobles. Wylder is the main man in charge, Kaige helps him lay down the law, Gideon covers the tech side, and Rowan can negotiate anyone under a table."

The affection in his voice was unmistakable. I looked over the four men—all of them tough and assured, but otherwise very different.

Kaige was the largest, a little bigger and broader even than Logan with a sheen of dark hair on his scalp and a twinkle in his eyes that suggested he wasn't actually that scary as long as you didn't piss him off. Wylder was almost as tall but not quite as brawny, looking slick in his collared shirt and dark jeans but with fiery auburn hair that I had a feeling from his fierce expression matched his temperament.

The tech expert, Gideon, was slim though toned, almost delicate-looking, but he offset that impression with the bold blue of his dyed hair and his sharply penetrating gaze. And Rowan—I never would have guessed he was part of a street gang with his business casual button-up and slacks, his blond hair combed neatly back. But at Mercy's mention of the threat to Beckett, his face had momentarily darkened with a hint of brutal protectiveness.

"We're here to take this asshole down," Wylder said without a trace of doubt. "Whatever it takes."

"Yep." Kaige cracked his knuckles—and then cracked a grin as well. "And then maybe we can get to know Beckett's new friends with a whole lot less explosions and gunfire going around. We know how to have fun—the not-so-bloody kind—too."

His gaze veered to Slade's lower leg, where the other guy had propped it at an angle that revealed a sliver of his prosthetic above his typical neon sneakers. "Looks like you've already been through a war or two."

"Oh, this?" Slade drawled. "Crazy story, actually. My grandma went on this insane rampage when I was a kid—"

"He was born like that," I cut him off, hitting him in the arm. "And he's fine, before anyone asks."

Slade clucked his tongue at me, but his eyes glittered with silent laughter. "You take the fun out of everything, Piccolina."

"I'm just trying to keep us on topic," I told him with an affectionate bump of my elbow. "We do have an actual war to fight, as soon as possible."

Dexter nodded, his gaze pensive as he took in our new allies, flitting from one to the next without holding eye contact for more than an instant. "We have the manpower now—how are we going to use it to stop Doom's Seed? So far we haven't managed to do much more than fend off and avoid his attacks."

Beckett's smile vanished, his mouth settling into a hard line. "We've been discussing that… and I think it's time to go straight to the source. We've tried to work around Doom's Seed's offensives while searching for evidence for long enough. We go at him in one big move and rip the evidence we need right from him."

"What exactly does that mean?" Logan asked.

Beckett folded his arms over his chest. "First, we need to identify his main base of operations in this state. That's where the key materials will be. And between my tech guys, Gideon's genius, and your skills, I'm hoping it won't take long at all tp track down that location. If you're up for a little collaboration."

Logan glanced at Gideon, and one corner of his lips curved upward in a crooked smirk. "I think I can handle that. Let's get down to work."

———

I hadn't realized how quickly the techies could work once they combined their skills. In the mid-afternoon,

Logan and Gideon called us into Beckett's rooms to go over their findings. The room was big enough that even with my four guys, Mercy and her four, and me all clustered around the sitting area, it didn't feel crowded.

Gideon brought up a map on his tablet. "Here we are, and here's the building we've determined that Doom's Seed is running the majority of his local operations out of." He pointed to a pin marking a spot quite a distance away in a different city.

The same city where Yvonne had taken me when she'd kidnapped me, I recognized.

"It's not the condo Logan's mom brought me to, is it?" I said, startled. I hadn't noticed much activity while I was there, but then, I had been shut in a closet for most of that time.

Logan shook his head. "No, it's at the other end of the city, but the presence of the condo helped us narrow things down." He smiled tightly. "Her kidnapping attempt worked against Doom's Seed in more ways than one."

"We've found the place," Dexter said. "But if that location is important to Doom's Seed, he'll have a lot of his people guarding it, won't he? And they'll have the advantage of being on familiar ground. We can't just lay siege there in the middle of the city for days on end."

My mind leapt to the memory of how we'd tackled the enemy forces when they'd had Beckett's people under siege. "We create some kind of distraction nearby to draw as many of them away as possible. He doesn't know we've located his main base, and we've never gone directly after him unprovoked before. He might not even realize it has anything to do with us."

"Especially since there's new blood in the mix." Wylder grinned and rubbed his hands together. "His people aren't familiar with ours, and we've got the manpower to keep them busy for a while. You five have a better idea what you're looking for. I say we divide and conquer."

Mercy's eyes lit up in anticipation. "Perfect. I'll take the Claws to one part of the city, you take the Nobles to another, and Beckett can bring his people to the base once it's less guarded."

Gideon motioned to the tablet. "We also identified a few major businesses Doom's Seed is running in the same city. Those would make ideal targets. We pick two that are far apart and not very close to the base, and that should divide his force."

Beckett inhaled slowly. "All right. We don't want too big a commotion at the base, or Doom's Seed will catch wind of our plan and call his people back. I'll bring a small squad of Storm people who are loyal to me and…"

He looked at me and hesitated. "This is going to be the most dangerous mission we've carried out—riskier than anything you've been a part of before."

I could already see where he was going with this. I narrowed my eyes at him. "Don't you dare suggest that I lounge around here painting my toenails while you and the other guys go charging into danger."

Beckett held up his hands. "I have to try. It'll be

easier for me not having to worry about you getting hurt."

I raised my eyebrows. "And you won't be worried if I'm back here with hardly anyone left guarding the house? Doom's Seed already threatened to attack you here too. At least this way you'll know I'm okay—I'll be right there grabbing the proof we need with you. You know I've put up a good fight before."

His mouth tightened, and Mercy rolled her eyes at him. "Come on, Beckett. I thought you knew better than to try to leave a woman out of the action. She's obviously made of strong stuff if she's stuck with you this far."

Beckett's gaze jerked to her, dark with stormy emotion. "She isn't just *a* woman. She's *my* woman." He paused and let out a sigh. "And that means I support her choices even when I don't totally like them." He caught my gaze. "I'm sorry. I had to say it."

I gave him a half-hearted glower. "Just don't say it again. You don't have to like it, but I'm not leaving you guys to do this alone."

"None of us are staying back," Logan said emphatically, for once not joining Beckett on the over-protective side of things. I guessed he'd learned his lesson. He rubbed his mouth, considering the map. "And if we can find my mom while we're there, I can use that to our advantage. With whatever influence I have left with her, I'll gather any information I can."

My pulse stuttered. I hadn't thought about him

having to come face to face with Yvonne again. "Do you have any idea where she's been staying?"

His gaze was pained when he met my eyes. "No. As far as we can tell, she hasn't been back to the condo building since you escaped. We haven't been able to trace her movements since then."

She could be anywhere. There was no reason to assume we'd encounter her. But she was deeply entwined with Doom's Seed, and this was his primary center of operations in the area.

We might even have to face off with Doom's Seed himself.

A chill ran through me, but I willed it away. It didn't matter how much danger we were facing. This man had destroyed my family, attacked my mom and my men, and been ready to kill me at the drop of a hat. I wasn't letting him get away with any of that, no matter what I had to do.

"All right. We're agreed, then." Beckett drew himself straighter, looking around at all of us. "I hate that the situation has come to this—I hate that more people may die today. But all of us have been through the wringer with people who think they can control us and claim our territory. It doesn't matter what tactics our enemy has been willing to use or what threats he's made, I know we'll come out on top. All Doom's Seed cares about is his business, but we're fighting for something much more valuable."

His gaze flicked to me, and then around over the others again. "We're fighting for family."

Kaige let out a little whoop of approval, and Slade offered a brief round of applause. Tears pricked behind my eyes at the sentiment.

I couldn't help seeing how we all marched out of the room with an extra pep in our step, buoyed up by Beckett's words.

He'd come into his own as a leader in every possible way, no matter what his dad had to say about it. No matter how much the old Storm disapproved of his son's choices.

I couldn't say for sure that we'd come out of this final battle unscathed, but with Beckett at the helm, our chances couldn't have been better.

CHAPTER
TWENTY-THREE

Logan

The modest two-story brick building stood stark against the sinking evening sun. I stared up at it through the window of our car from where we were parked down the street. A heavy mix of trepidation and apprehension churned in my stomach.

This was it, our final gambit. If we couldn't find something that would destroy Doom's Seed in his base of operations, then he'd essentially won.

In the driver's seat, Beckett tapped at his phone's screen. "All right," he told the rest of us. "My people dealt with the guards who stayed back after most of the people stationed here took off to tackle the Claws and the Nobles. They haven't seen anyone else in or around the place, although they have a limited view of the interior. We still have to be very careful."

I nodded, touching the pistol tucked into the waistband of my jeans. "I'm ready. We go in now?"

"The faster we get in there, the more time we have before the men my friends diverted return."

Beckett shoved his phone into his pocket and pushed open his door, and the rest of us spilled out after him. Maddie's pale hair swished over her shoulders as she raised her chin defiantly.

A pang of love shot through my chest. She was here standing with us right until the end. She really was an incredible woman.

I had to make sure this asshole could never hurt her or anyone she cared about again.

Dexter strode ahead of us, checking the front door and then hustling around to the back. As we came down the lane beside the building to join him, he returned, frowning.

"He's got some high-tech locks on the doors. I can't open them with my typical tools."

"Let's see." Slade marched down the lane and spun to take in the rear of the building. He let out a chuckle. "They were so focused on the doors, they didn't think about the windows."

He pointed to a large window on the second floor which was standing open to let in the warm spring air. The windows on the first floor were barred, but not those above. And a dumpster stood against the back of the building just close enough that we could use it to get us most of the way there.

I eyeballed it. "I'll boost you all up and then I should be able to reach it on my own. Or you can give me a hand from above."

The others nodded without a word. We all knew there wasn't time for arguing if one of us came up with a solid enough plan. We just needed to get inside.

We scrambled onto the dumpster, me helping Dexter when he wobbled. Not wanting to send Maddie through first, I gave Beckett a leg up. He pushed on the screen, and it popped out with a faint clatter on the floor in the room above. He scrambled inside.

I hefted up Slade and Dexter and finally Maddie, giving her a quick kiss first. She touched my cheek. "I'll be fine."

"I'm going to make sure of that," I told her, and boosted her to where she could grip the window ledge.

Standing with my arms stretched as high as they could go, I couldn't quite touch the ledge by myself. But after bending my knees, I managed to spring high enough to hook my hands over it. Slade and Beckett leaned out to grab my arms, supporting my weight as I clambered farther inside and then backing up to give me room to ease in.

We'd come into a bedroom where a few of Doom's Seed's men must have slept, cots lining the walls with a mess of clothing draped across their frames.

"No sign of anyone so far," Beckett said under his breath. "We all know the drill."

"I'll start downstairs," I said, since it looked like the upstairs might be more living space than work area.

My job was to find a computer, any computer, and gain access so we could steal all the files these people were keeping on it. The others were searching out physical evidence—paper records or anything else that could contribute to a case or give us leverage.

Whether we got the cops involved after all or we forced Doom's Seed to back off on our own, I didn't care. I just wanted this mess over with.

Maddie and Slade followed me down the stairs while Beckett and Dexter split off to check the upstairs rooms. Knowing Slade would have Maddie's back, I let myself hurry ahead of them since I could scan the rooms more quickly for my target. My pistol stayed in my hand, ready in case we encountered anyone.

There was a living room of sorts with a mix of clashing armchairs, a dining room with a big scratched up table, and a room that appeared to be used for storage with loads of cardboard boxes and crates. Slade and Maddie started digging through the containers there, but I hadn't seen a single computer yet.

At least we also hadn't run into any adversaries either.

I pushed into another room and found a couple of desks, a filing cabinet, a bookcase stacked with odds and ends... and a laptop sitting smack in the middle of one of the desks.

"Bingo," I murmured, and then raised my voice to

carry across the hall. "There's an office room here that could have some useful records."

"We'll check it out as soon as we've gone through this crap," Slade called back.

I sat on the edge of the desk with my back to the wall where I could easily keep an eye on the door and popped open the laptop. A window came up asking for a password.

Okay, time to get to work. I set my gun on the desk next to the computer and dove in.

My fingers darted over the keyboard, opening up the functions that would let me bypass the protection. I was about halfway through the sequence when a thump carried from upstairs, followed by a shout.

A shout in a female voice. Not Maddie's, but one I recognized.

It was Mom's.

I froze for an instant with a lurch of my heart, and then I threw myself off the desk, tucking the laptop under my arm.

I hurtled up the stairs, racing as fast as my pulse, and only slowed to get my bearings when I reached the upper hall. Beckett's low, even voice was carrying from a doorway near the end. "I don't want to hurt you. We're here to *stop* anyone else from getting hurt."

A scoffing sound answered him, wordless but with enough of a voice to it that I knew it was my mother. I hurried down the hall.

When I reached the doorway, I stalled in my tracks, my heart stuttering all over again.

The large room was set up like a combination bedroom and study. A queen-sized bed with a sleigh bedframe and matching oak vanity stood at one end. A heavy bookcase full of tomes that looked like they belonged in the university library stood against the wall across from the door. A narrow desk squatted kitty-corner from it.

Mom was poised by the foot of the bed, her hands raised but her mouth twisted into a sneer. Beckett had only come a couple of steps into the room. He was pointing his gun straight at her.

It was impossible to fully describe the barrage of emotions that swept through me at the sight of my mom—in general and in that position. Part of me wanted to run to her protection, even now. Part of me wanted to yell at her that she deserved Beckett's hostility after everything she'd done. Horror and loss and anger and the slightest flicker of hope all whirled inside me.

Beckett's gaze never left her, but he'd obviously noted my arrival. "I won't shoot her as long as she doesn't force the issue, Logan."

From the stone-cold expression on Mom's face, it was possible she would. She might be considering leaping at him and wrestling him for the gun, and I doubted that would have ended well.

But then her gaze slid to me, and a little shiver ran through her. Her lips pulled back from their flat line into a pained frown.

She still cared, at least a little.

I had to use that sliver of concern, not let it win me

over. Maybe there could be some kind of reconciliation down the line, but not anytime soon.

Her hands were empty, no sign of weapons protruding from her fitted slacks or silk blouse. If she had anything in her pockets, it couldn't be very large.

I took a gamble, set the laptop on the desk by the door, and approached her with slow, careful steps. Her eyes widened, a hint of moisture shimmering in them.

"Logan," Beckett said in a warning tone, but he didn't move to stop me. I was careful not to step into his line of fire. I didn't trust this woman anywhere near *that* much.

When I was close enough, Mom raised her hand to touch my cheek. I stopped, swallowing thickly as her fingertips grazed my skin.

"My boy," she murmured. "It is good to see you again, even like this."

She didn't want to hurt me. Maybe I was the only person that could be said about other than Doom's Seed.

I had to do this. I had to try. Even if it sent a jab of guilt through my gut in spite of everything.

I turned back toward Beckett, which also happened to angle me so that my hip pocket with my phone was blocked from Mom's view. I tugged it out surreptitiously, just far enough to tap the controls I needed, and tucked it back inside in the space of a few seconds.

"Leave us alone," I said at the same time. "I need to talk to my mom privately, just the two of us."

Beckett hesitated, even though I knew he'd caught my move with the phone and probably guessed what I was doing. "Logan, are you sure—?"

"Yes," I interrupted. "It's fine. There are some things we should keep between family."

His jaw clenched, but then he inclined his head. "All right. I'll keep searching the building." He cut his gaze toward Mom. "You'd better tell me now if there's anyone else I might run into here, because I won't be as careful with my gun around *his* people."

Mom shook her head. "It's just me and the guards who were outside. I assume you're already aware of them, whatever happened to them."

Beckett narrowed his eyes like he wasn't sure he believed her, and I wasn't sure I did either. But he backed out of the room and shut the door behind him.

Perfect. The more private Mom thought this conversation was, the better.

My fingers itched for the pistol I'd left downstairs, but I didn't think it would have set the mood here very well anyway. I had to act like I had more faith in Mom than I actually did if this maneuver was going to work.

I pulled my gaze back to Mom, backing up half a step to give myself more room to breathe—and to take in any telling gestures. "Mom, you have to realize it's over now. We're coming down on Doom's Seed hard. He's not getting away with any of this."

Mom's shoulders stiffened. "You shouldn't be messing around in—"

"*You* shouldn't have gotten involved in his mess," I

shot back. "I still don't get it. How could you have thought that going to a crime lord for an illegally obtained organ was the best thing for me? Do you even know how he got that liver?"

"No," Mom said defiantly. "I have no idea, and I don't care. It saved your life—*he* saved your life—and that matters more than the red tape."

"Someone could have been *murdered* for him to have it. Doesn't that matter to you? I don't understand how you could have not only done that, but also gotten so involved with him that you'd fake your death and leave me and Dad behind to be with him instead."

"I told you on the phone, you don't know what my life was like." She sounded more choked up than angry saying it now, though. Her gaze dropped to the floor and returned to my face. "I've wished I could see you, talk to you, for so long. I hated leaving you behind. But it was the only way I could protect everyone I cared about. If anyone had found out the truth about your operation, it could have ruined your life too."

"Don't pretend you ran away *for* me," I said. "You told me that you weren't happy with Dad. Fine. But hooking up with a vicious mafia boss—seriously?"

"You don't know him. There's so much about him that you don't know."

"I know enough." I folded my arms over my chest. "Have you been helping him now—going out there and arranging for these organs to come in, finding people desperate enough to pay him for them?"

"No!" she insisted. "*He* doesn't even get that

involved. He just gives the orders, and his people look for the marks. He's barely a part of it at all."

"He threatened to kill Maddie. He *did* order his people to kill her dad."

Mom grimaces. "That was an unavoidable precaution, or everything would have fallen apart. It's not as if I wanted to see Evan Silver dead, but if it was him or you…"

"And Doom's Seed," I filled in.

She just stared at me, her expression tight but her body trembling just slightly.

I had everything I could have wanted now. Comments confirming that the man who called himself Doom's Seed had illegally supplied my liver, had an ongoing business for arranging transplants, and had orchestrated at least one specific murder, all recorded in my mom's voice on my phone. She had no idea, and prickles of guilt were still nagging at my insides, but I'd done what was necessary.

Now I had to give her a chance to get herself out of this mess before it imploded around her.

I lowered my voice. "It's all going to end now, Mom. We're going to bring justice down on him, and anyone standing with him will fall too. It's time to do the right thing. You probably wouldn't even face any jail time if you agreed to testify against him about the things you've seen."

Mom outright shuddered. "I couldn't do that. I *love* him, Logan. We're in this together, me and him, come hell or high water."

I held her gaze. "Shouldn't you be able to say that about your own son? Isn't it time that you were here for me again? Walk away from this with me, please. You can divorce Dad properly, live life however you want it, in a way that won't put everyone around you under threat."

"Logan…" Her voice broke with emotion.

I pushed my advantage. "I want you in my life. I want to get what we should have had. Do you have any idea how much I missed you all those years?"

Mom blinked hard. She swiped at her eyes and took a step toward me. "I've missed you so much too, sweetheart. When I think about all the time I've lost with you, it kills me. I don't know—"

Her words were cut off by the thump of the bookcase swinging from the wall. I only had an instant to register that the bookcase had been concealing a hidden doorway when a broad-shouldered, graying man in a vibrant peacock-blue suit burst from the opening into the room.

He was holding a pistol pointed straight at me. As I jerked backward, my pulse skittering, he barreled toward me, and it clicked in the back of my startled, panicked mind that this must be Doom's Seed.

"He's your weakness, Yvonne," he growled. "The only one you have left, and I'm going to eliminate him. Then you'll really be free."

His finger closed around the trigger—and as I wrenched myself to the side, Mom dove in front of him.

"No!" she cried out just as the gun boomed. Her good hand had snatched something from her pocket and plunged it at him, but in the same moment pain tore across my shoulder.

The bullet had gone wide, but not wide enough. Doom's Seed and I stumbled in opposite directions, me toward the bed, him toward the bookcase. The gun slipped from his fingers.

He clapped a hand against his side, where he was bleeding… because of the blood streaked blade my mom was still clutching in her white-knuckled hand.

Mom had stabbed him. Mom had interrupted his shot and attacked the man she said she loved in her attempt to save me.

But as blood coursed down my sleeve from the burning wound that had my left arm sagging, I wasn't sure it'd been enough.

CHAPTER
TWENTY-FOUR

Madelyn

was just stepping out of the storage room ahead of Slade when a gunshot blared through the building. My nerves jumped with a jolt of panic.

Without a word, both me and Slade took off for the stairs. Thudding footsteps behind us told me that at least one other of my guys was hurtling after us.

Where had the shot come from? Who had been shooting at whom? Had any of my guys been injured?

The frantic thoughts propelled me up the stairs and into the upstairs hall. A thump from a room farther down told me where to go. I dashed toward the doorway with Slade at my heels.

We barged into the room and jerked to a halt. It

took me a few seconds to take in the scene in front of me and make any kind of sense of it.

Yvonne was standing almost directly in front of me, a bloody knife clutched in her regular hand, her body braced in a defensive stance. At her left, a man with gray hair and a flashy suit had sagged back against a large bookcase—which was pulled away from the wall to reveal a hidden doorway. He was clutching his side, where blood streaked from a wound on his belly. Yvonne's gaze was fixed on him as if she was worried about what he'd do next.

At her left, Logan was slouched near the room's bed. He leaned against the footboard while his other hand pressed to his shoulder—where *his* blood was coursing down his arm.

I couldn't suppress a yelp of alarm. At the same moment, Beckett burst into the room. He slipped between me and Slade with his pistol raised. His aim swung toward the man in the flashy suit the second he set eyes on him.

"Doom's Seed," he bit out. "Seems like the tables have turned just a little, don't you think?"

This was Doom's Seed. And Yvonne had stabbed him? Who had hurt Logan?

What the hell was going on?

Before my whirling mind could figure it out, Yvonne ducked down. She dropped the knife and snatched something else off the floor—a gun that had fallen. And the pieces clicked together.

Doom's Seed must have shot at Logan, but Yvonne had tried to protect him.

Clearly she wasn't totally turning against her lover, though. She lifted the gun and stepped between him and Beckett, protecting the man she'd just stabbed. Her hands shook, the prosthetic one supporting the one gripping the gun, but her face hardened.

"I'm sorry, my love," she said to the man she was shielding. "I—you came at him so quickly—I had to protect him—"

"Fucking bitch," Doom's Seed muttered, and Yvonne winced. But she didn't waver from her position in front of him.

She motioned at Beckett with the gun, and Beckett backed up one step, his jaw tightening. "You made the right choice with your first response," he said. "Don't screw it up now."

"Leave him alone," she snapped back. "If you try to hurt him, I'll shoot all of you. I don't care what happens to me."

My heart thudded at an anxious pace. I eased toward Logan and, when Yvonne's attention didn't leave Beckett, hurried the rest of the way to my stepbrother. His startled gaze shifted from his mom to me.

"She saved me," he mumbled.

"Not completely. Let me see that."

Bracing himself, he lifted his hand from the wound. I sucked in a breath of dismay. The bullet had only clipped his shoulder, but deeply enough to leave a thick gouge through the muscle. Blood streamed down from it before my eyes.

Logan focused on me more steadily. "I'm okay."

"You *will* be okay once I get the bleeding stopped," I said, putting on my best medical professional voice and tuning out my panic. "It's deep, and it'll leave a scar, but it hasn't hit anything vital."

I groped around for something to bandage the wound and grabbed the two pillows from the head of the bed. Once I'd yanked both of the pillowcases off them, I folded one into a thick pad that I pressed against Logan's shoulder and tied it in place with the other as firmly as I could.

His head bowed toward mine, his mouth almost brushing my cheek. "I got everything we need. It's all good."

I had no idea what he was talking about, but I couldn't focus only on him. Doom's Seed had started chuckling as he pushed himself straighter against the doorframe.

"Do you really think I'm finished now, boy?" he spat at Beckett. "You're going to regret every second you spent challenging me."

"Me challenging *you*?" Beckett said incredulously. "You're the one who's rampaged through my territory and tried to destroy my reputation. I might be young, but I've been raised to become the Storm since the day I was born, and you'd better believe I won't stand back while my empire is threatened."

Doom's Seed snorted. "*Your* empire? I hardly think

so, especially after the conversation I had with your father. Now, he's a man who knows what's good for him."

"Then it's a good thing he's not the one really in charge anymore, isn't it?" Beckett's eyes glinted with anger. "Withdraw now and give all your territory in this state over to me, and *maybe* I'll overlook all those transgressions. Otherwise, it'll be your empire in ashes."

"I'll believe it when I see it," the other man said disdainfully. He pointed a thick finger at Beckett from where he was still slumped against the bookcase, his arm steadier than I'd have expected. "You haven't mastered this business yet. You haven't earned the throne. I have all the power here."

Beckett gave a rough laugh, and my pulse hiccupped at the twitch of Yvonne's hands. She still had the gun aimed directly at Beckett's chest, but he didn't show the slightest sign of worry.

"Are you kidding me?" he said. "You haven't been fighting this battle with my dad. You've been fighting it with me, and you know it. *Everybody* knows it. But you've never been man enough to come directly to me to work out shit. You target my friends. My *dad*. That's not strong. It's pathetic."

Doom's Seed glowered at him. "It's a strategy. One you'll need to learn if you haven't already. Until you shed your weaknesses, you'll always be a weak little boy. Now get out of my sight before—"

A figure sprang through the doorway with a shout, gun brandished. I had only an instant to recognize him as one of the Storm men Beckett had brought along before a bang split my eardrums.

But it wasn't from his gun. Yvonne swayed with the recoil of her shot, her pistol immediately jerking back toward Beckett, and the guy in the doorway crumpled. The top of his head was nothing more than a mash of flesh, blood, and shards of skull.

My stomach lurched. "Don't look," Logan gritted out, as if I could heed the warning now.

I dragged my gaze back to Yvonne, a sharper queasiness welling up inside me.

She wasn't just posturing with the gun. She was totally prepared to use it—and her aim was good.

"Mom," Logan said, his voice still strained, but it was Doom's Seed who answered him.

"Don't go guilting your mother," the older man snarled. "No fucking respect. Aren't you grateful that she arranged for me to save your life?"

Logan stared right back at him. "I'd rather have died than have someone else die in my place who didn't need to."

Yvonne's mouth twisted, and at the same moment, I noticed Slade creeping around the edge of the room. He looked like he was getting into position to lunge at Yvonne, maybe hoping to grab the gun. But he only got halfway there before she pulled out of her momentary distraction and caught the movement too.

"Get back by the door," she snapped at him with a wave of the gun.

Slade froze and slowly eased backward again. Then

Yvonne's attention whipped to Dexter. "And you. Whatever you've got behind your back, toss it down the stairs."

Dexter froze where he'd been reaching behind himself. Frowning, he stepped backward and tossed something that clattered down the steps—some kind of weapon, I had to assume.

Doom's Seed pushed himself all the way onto his feet with only a brief grimace. Yvonne's gaze flicked back toward him, but not for long enough for any of us to take advantage. Seeing him mobile, her lips pursed.

Abruptly, she gestured with the gun at all of us. "Out of the room! Every one of you. Out of the goddamn building, as fast as you can go, *now*!"

When we stalled, gaping at her, she stomped her foot on the floor. "Now, or I'm going to start shooting." She glanced at Logan. "I don't feel any need to protect your friends, especially after all the trouble they've created for us."

Every muscle in my body balked at the idea of giving up, but I couldn't see how to get the upper hand.

Logan gripped my arm with a meaningful squeeze. "We'll go," he said. "No need to shoot anyone else."

He caught my gaze, and I remembered abruptly what he'd said about having everything we needed. Had he already dug up files that could end the conflict from Doom's Seed's computer or found some other evidence that would definitively turn the tide?

I had to trust him. He'd been part of the

confrontation with his mom from the start—he knew what he was doing.

I nodded and started to walk with him.

Beckett stepped to the side of the door with a pained glance at his fallen employee. "You all go out ahead of me. I'll bring up the rear, just to make sure these two don't try anything stupid."

I smiled tightly at him with a wave of gratitude. Please, let this be enough. Please, let it be over.

Slade and Dexter, who were closest to the door, filed out first. I nudged Logan ahead of me, wanting to get him to safety as quickly as possible since he'd have trouble defending himself with his injury.

Doom's Seed shuffled a little forward. Beckett's gun bobbed toward him and then back to point at Yvonne. I gripped his shirt for just a second as I moved to pass him, a gesture of thanks and affection.

Just as my foot hit the threshold, Doom's Seed threw himself forward.

I spun around at the scuff of his footsteps and saw the glint of a metal blade in his hand—a blade he was stabbing straight at Beckett. He must have been counting on surprise to reach Beckett before Beckett could react and shoot him.

He wanted to end this conflict too—with one of the men I loved dead at his feet.

And maybe he would have succeeded, but my instincts honed by my Krav Maga classes kicked in. Without thinking, I hurled myself between the two men.

My elbow shot out, catching Doom's Seed in the neck twice as hard with the force of his momentum. He let out a choking sound and stumbled backward but then slashed out with the knife—this time toward me.

I ducked and kicked out, and my gaze snagged on another blade, right within reach. The small, blood-stained one Yvonne had set down on the floor after picking up the gun.

"Stop!" she shrieked as I snatched it up, but Doom's Seed was lunging at us again, blocking any chance of a clear shot. She wouldn't risk hitting him.

I had no such qualms.

He was on top of me, the knife raking over my side as he fumbled for a better blow. One more second, and I was a goner. So I did what I had to do to save my life and possibly Beckett's too.

I couldn't reach his neck at this angle, but I knew from all my medical studies exactly where to plunge that blade into his chest to stop the beating of his heart. I slammed it home with all the strength I had in me.

If this man survived, he'd only hurt more people. Kill more people. I couldn't let that happen. He was a disease, and I was cutting him out of this world.

I shoved the blade in deeper, and Doom's Seed collapsed over me with a gush of blood.

"Maddie!" Beckett cried out, crouching with me, but I could already tell the body slumped over me was vacant of life.

As I squirmed out from under Doom's Seed's heavy

corpse with a ragged breath, Yvonne dropped to her knees at his other side.

"No," she said between sobs, groping at his wound as if she could bring him back. "No, no, no."

But Doom's Seed didn't so much as twitch as I staggered to my feet. He was gone.

Madelyn

Slade flopped down at one end of the sofa in Beckett's sitting room with an exaggerated sigh. "Well, I think I've talked to enough cops to last me for the next century or so."

Logan sat next to him, careful of his newly stitched-up shoulder. "No kidding."

"It was necessary," I pointed out, but I couldn't restrain a yawn as I sank down at the far end of the sofa, letting my legs sprawl across Logan's lap. My eyes felt heavy, my head muggy.

It'd been a long couple of days. After figuring out our story and calling the cops to the scene of Doom's Seed's death, we'd all been in and out of questioning since yesterday evening, other than a brief reprieve back here to get a little sleep. Not that any of us had felt all that inclined to relax.

Beckett had managed to stay mostly on the sidelines, presenting himself as a concerned friend. We'd offered up our evidence from across the Vigil's investigation, including Logan's recording of his mom confessing her knowledge of some of Doom's Seed's criminal activities. In her emotional state, Yvonne had ended up admitting more to the cops than probably would have been wise if she'd been thinking clearly.

I glanced over at Logan. "It seems like your mom will be going away for a while."

He shrugged, though I could tell from the tensing of his jaw that he still had complicated feelings about the woman who'd raised him for the first several years of his life. "It's what she deserves. Maybe she'll get herself sorted out while she's in there… or maybe she's a lost cause. Either way, at least the truth is out."

Beckett stopped by the side of the sofa and looked down at us. "Speaking of the truth, did you find out why the cops were after you guys the other day?"

Dexter perched on one of the armchairs as he answered. "Doom's Seed must have had the manager at the Fresh Catch Seafood Market call in a complaint that we'd broken in and stolen something. They were following up on that accusation, wanting to question us."

Beckett's eyebrows rose. "But the police aren't bringing charges?"

Slade snorted. "It was all hearsay. They didn't have

any proof. We said we snooped around a bit while the market was open to explain the pics Dex had of the shipping containers, but there's nothing illegal about walking into a back room without even touching anything."

"And they were too excited about getting to take a huge criminal kingpin down to be very worried about a little petty larceny anyway," I added wryly, and tipped my head back against the arm of the sofa. "We are going to have to testify in court once the cases against Logan's mom and some of Doom's Seed's top dogs go to trial."

Slade dismissed my remark with a wave of his hand. "Not for a while. We'll be totally recovered by then and ready for it. Especially now that this crazy case is off our plates."

Beckett focused on me. "You're not in any trouble over stabbing Doom's Seed, are you?"

I shook my head. "It was clear self-defense. I have the bruises and scratches to show he attacked me, and he'd already shot Logan—Yvonne confirmed that even if they hadn't believed us. I guess the scene must have shown a pretty obvious struggle too."

"Well, a whole lot of Doom's Seed's empire is about to crash and burn, with the organ transplant trade going first," Beckett said. "From what I hear, some of his people that the cops rounded up are already cutting deals, turning over evidence and testimony that'll implicate even more people and shady businesses."

"Good," I muttered. That'd always been the most important goal to me—knowing that I'd finished what

Dad had started and brought down the business that'd been exploiting so many people. Hopefully he could rest easier now, wherever his soul had departed to.

Logan ran his hand over my calf and started to massage my foot. I wanted to melt into his touch, but too many questions were still whirling through my mind.

I twisted at the waist to get a steadier look at Beckett. "Now that he's gone... who will the next Doom's Seed be? Do we have to worry about them picking up the pieces and starting over?"

"Or trying to get revenge for his death?" Dexter piped up.

Beckett rubbed his chin, his expression turning pensive. "I'm honestly not sure who'll step up. It's possible he had children, at least one of whom would have been raised to take over from him when necessary like my dad raised me. But even if it's someone with a personal stake, with the police so involved it'd be madness to try to attack any of you again. And I've shown that the Storm isn't anyone to be screwed over."

"What if he didn't have kids?" Logan asked.

"Then the Devil's Dozen will confer about who to offer the position to. It could be we'll decide an associate of his could fill his shoes the best. Or we might invite someone totally new to take his spot at the table. Either way, I'll have some say on the subject since I'm officially taking over as the Storm now. No matter how my dad feels about it."

His voice hardened a bit with that last sentence. I

shot him a reassuring smile. "I know you'll be amazing at it."

He'd make sure to pick someone who wouldn't try to resurrect the worst parts of Doom's Seed's empire. Beckett had been with me every step of the way, and he'd seen the conflict through to the end, no matter how dangerous it'd gotten for his own family legacy.

A wave of emotion washed over me, and tears welled up in my eyes. "It's finally over," I said, swiping at them. "We can get back to our regular lives without this hanging over us." The cops had already escorted Mom, Holand, and Summer back to their homes—well, in Mom and Holand's case, to a more local hotel while they sorted out the insurance from the house and decided whether to rebuild or buy something new.

We were all going to get to rebuild now, in our own various ways. And the five of us could build something *together*, enjoying the trust and loyalty we'd found with each other.

I reached out to squeeze Logan's forearm and let my gaze travel over all four of my guys. "I'm so happy to be here with you. I can't wait to see how good life can be once we can focus on simply living it."

"Cheers to that," Slade said with a grin, and my guys closed in around me in a joint embrace.

CHAPTER
TWENTY-SIX

One year later

Madelyn

omehow Summer always managed to have perfect timing. I was just walking into the house when my phone pinged with an incoming text.

Inhaling the lingering floral scent from the wax burner Mom had given me as a housewarming gift, I pulled my phone out of my purse.

You've got to be home by now, Summer had written. *How did the presentation go? I need all the deets!*

I grinned and started tapping my thumbs as I

kicked off the low-heeled pumps I'd worn for this semi-formal occasion. *The presentation went amazing. I still can't believe I got the opportunity at all! I'll have to thank Prof. Fernandez again… especially because I may have scored the most awesome summer internship in existence!*

OMG, what? Summer wrote back an instant later. *Don't leave your bestie hanging.*

My grin only grew as I answered. *Jamie Harvey from Harvey Labs attended the talk—that's the medical research facility I was telling you about that just won an international award for innovation. Afterward, he came up to me, told me he was impressed by my talk, and gave me his card telling me he'd love to have me interning at the lab this summer.*

I was still high from that accomplishment. The thought of all the things I might learn and get to be a part of in just a couple of months had me giddy.

That's fantastic! We need to go out and celebrate ASAP. I have some good news too, but not as big as yours. My date last night with the new guy was pretty spectacular.

My eyebrows shot up. *Don't tell me you've actually found someone you want to go on a second date with. That's front-page news!*

Summer sent a laughing and a tongue-sticking-out emoji in response, and I laughed to myself.

I've got to get back to work—break's just about over—but I'll call you tonight and fill you in, she wrote back.

I tucked my phone away and set my shoes on the mat in the front hall next to Dexter's loafers and Slade's spare pair of sneakers—neon yellow, naturally. Looking at them together, breathing in the scent I was just starting to associate with home, a softer smile crossed my face.

Just having this place, which we'd only moved into a couple of months ago, was pretty amazing. We'd only been able to afford the five-bedroom because of Beckett's significant financial contribution, but he'd insisted on the investment, saying it was a drop in the bucket for him.

Living with all four of my guys was fantastic. There was nothing better than coming out of my bedroom in the morning and getting to steal a good morning kiss— or a few—within seconds. Sometimes before I even left the bedroom.

The clinking of pots and utensils drew me into the kitchen: modest-sized but decked out with high-end appliances that Dexter had practically swooned over. A spicy, savory scent tickled my nose before I'd even reached the doorway, setting my mouth watering.

I found my culinarily-inclined boyfriend standing by the stove, stirring something in a sauté pan while two other pots bubbled merrily and something sizzled faintly from within the oven.

"Looks like you've been busy," I said, walking over and judging his response before reaching out for physical contact. When he leaned a little toward me in welcome, I slipped my arm around his waist and pecked him on the cheek.

Dexter beamed at me. "I figured a feast was in order. You had that big presentation—and the internship offer to celebrate too—and Beckett's getting back from his trip to hash out that huge business deal."

"We could have just ordered in," I teased him, knowing exactly what response I'd get.

He let out a huff of mock offense and adjusted the heat dial for one of the burners. "You're never getting a meal as custom-tailored to everyone's tastes with takeout. And I needed the mental break from my final essay anyway."

I laughed lightly and gave him an affectionate squeeze before letting him go again. "I'm sure we can find other ways to distract you if the cooking isn't enough."

He shot me a sly glance before returning to his work, and I found myself remembering my first rehearsal of my presentation with the guys looking on. Slade had acted out the advice "picture the audience naked" to a literal extreme… with interesting results that had definitely loosened me up.

A blush tingled across my cheeks. I glanced across the counter and noticed a few tomatoes sitting on the cutting board. "Do you need these cut up? I can pitch in."

Dexter looked between me and the tomatoes hesitantly, likely weighing the risks of me cutting them incorrectly by his standards, before he nodded and passed me a knife. I positioned the tomato in front of me on the board and sliced it down the middle.

"Have you heard from Beckett today?" I asked. "I

texted him about the internship but haven't gotten a reply."

"He texted about an hour ago saying he'd just gotten in at the airport. I'm sure he'd have let you know too, but he was probably worried he'd interrupt your presentation. Maybe he's waiting to congratulate you in person." Dexter's gaze tracked my motions with the knife, and his mouth twitched. "Here, let me show you a more effective approach."

I suppressed a giggle as he came behind me and placed a hand over each of mine. He really liked having all the control in the kitchen, and I wouldn't critique him for it. Instead, I leaned back into his warmth as he guided my hand through the motions of cutting the tomatoes in a completely different way that he considered more effective. Which, knowing how conscientious he was, was probably true.

When we were finished, he dipped his head to press a scorching kiss to the nape of my neck. Then he nudged me toward the two stools at the kitchen's small island. "That's enough help after all the work you did today. You can sit and watch."

I gave him a mock salute and hopped onto one of the stools. I was just settling onto it when a key clicked in the front door's lock.

"It's me," Logan called out, a faint note of weariness in his voice that I only heard on days like today.

"We're in the kitchen," I said.

Moments later, my stepbrother strode through the doorway and made a beeline straight for me. He wrapped his brawny arms around me and hugged me tight, his head dipped close to mine.

I hugged him back, my throat constricting. "How was it?"

Logan sighed and pulled back just enough to rest his forehead against mine. "She's doing well, all things considered. We managed not to get into any arguments this time."

He'd made a habit of visiting his mom in prison every other week, and it seemed to help him cope with the disastrous turn their relationship had taken. He hadn't forgiven her for the crimes she'd been a part of or for abandoning him, but his residual anger had simmered down, so now he was mostly just sad. I knew from our talks that he no longer felt at all guilty about his role in putting her in jail.

It's where she belongs, he'd told me a few months ago. *And I can tell she's accepted that too. I guess that's some kind of progress.*

Logan's lips sought out mine, and I returned the kiss eagerly, our mouths melding together for the better part of a minute. When he drew back, I touched his cheek.

"Are you still meeting your dad for lunch tomorrow?" I asked.

He nodded, and his face lightened just a little bit. Joy sparked in my chest at the sight.

He'd become so much more relaxed about hanging out with Holand since the air had been cleared between them—and his dad hadn't shunned him the way he'd feared. We'd even gone to a larger family gathering for

Easter a few weekends ago, and it'd warmed my heart to see Logan ambling around chatting up all the relatives he'd spent most of the past few years avoiding.

I'd been able to tell from Holand's expression that he was even more pleased than I was.

Logan moved to the stove, snatching up a fork and spearing a mushroom out of the pan. He popped it into his mouth despite Dexter's disgruntled sound and then fanned his mouth to cool it off.

Dexter elbowed him. "What did you expect? I'm in the middle of cooking it—of course it's hot."

Logan smirked. "Delicious, though."

Dexter waved him off. "Why don't you make yourself useful and set the table?"

"I can do that."

I joined Logan in getting out the plates and glasses. We were just setting them out on the maple dining room table when Beckett appeared in the doorway.

"You're back! I didn't hear you come in." I hustled over to give him a hug and then a lingering kiss. I hadn't seen him in a few days—and his presence was always less consistent than my other men's. He still spent half his nights either at the Storm mansion or roving around to various other properties they owned looking after his empire.

"Glad to be here," Beckett said, nuzzling my hair. "Always my favorite place."

"You said the meeting went well?" Logan asked. "Exactly how well?"

Delight crinkled the corners of Beckett's eyes. "The

investors actually agreed to contribute *more* funding than I'd asked for. Which means we can add an extra wing to the building that I didn't think would even be possible."

"I'm not surprised," I told him. "You're very persuasive."

He chuckled and gave me another kiss. "And I hear you're on your way to earning your Nobel prize with this research internship."

I snorted. "I've got a lot more work to do before *that*. But I can't wait to get started."

Logan's phone pinged with an incoming text. He glanced at it. "Slade just got out of class. He should be here in ten minutes."

Dexter clapped his hands together. "Perfect timing. Let's get everything on the table."

He scooped the various delicacies out onto serving plates, which the rest of us carried into the dining room. Beckett pulled out two bottles of wine from the small collection he was building and got the chef to decide which was the better pairing. He was just filling the last of our glasses when Slade strode in.

"All this for me?" he joked, and slung his arm around my shoulders to pull me into a quick but ardent kiss. "Missed you, Piccolina."

"You just saw me this morning," I reminded him with a laugh.

"Any time without you is too long. But it looks like we'd better dig into this feast."

We all took our seats and grabbed portions from

each dish in the spread. There was chicken in a creamy sauce, rice mixed with various spices that turned it a vibrant shade of yellow, and three different types of vegetables with varied spicing.

I took one bite of the chicken and let out a moan at the sweet but tangy flavor. "You've outdone yourself again, Dex. I think this is my favorite yet."

He grinned. "I plan to keep topping myself as many times as I can."

"So…" Slade said, with a playful note in his voice that had us all turning toward him. "I was chatting with a couple of guys in one of my classes today and heard something interesting."

Now he had our undivided attention. "What's that?" I demanded before popping another bite of the incredible chicken into my mouth.

His dark eyes glinted with anticipation. "It seems like a couple of thugs have been trying to intimidate the one guy's parents at the art gallery they own. Trying to extort them with threats. And the cops have been totally useless at tracking the pricks down to make sure they don't follow through on those threats."

The hum of anticipation leapt from him to flow through all of us around the table. I sat up a little straighter, and Logan leaned forward. "I don't suppose they'd be happy to get a little outside help?"

Slade waggled his fork. "From what I gathered, they'd like nothing more."

Dexter's gaze had already gone distant as he started

working through logistics in his head. "I'm sure we'd be able to tackle a situation like that."

Beckett inclined his head. "And you've always got extra manpower from me if you need it."

The guys all glanced my way. I could have laughed at the question on their faces, as if they thought *I* was ever going to back down from the chance to deal out a little more justice in the world when the opportunity fell into our laps.

We were pretty darn great at being the Vigilante Kings—and Queen—and it would have been an awful shame if we'd totally retired.

I smiled back at all of them, my nerves already buzzing. "It sounds like a perfect new case for the Vigil to tackle. Let's finish with dinner and dive right in."

ABOUT THE AUTHORS

Eva Chance is a pen name for contemporary romance written by Amazon top 100 bestselling author Eva Chase. If you love gritty romance, dominant men, and fierce women who never have to choose, look no further.

Eva lives in Canada with her family. She loves stories both swoony and supernatural, and strong women and the men who appreciate them.

Connect with Eva online:
www.evachase.com
eva@evachase.com

Harlow King is a long-time fan of all things dark, edgy, and steamy. She can't wait to share her contemporary reverse harem stories.

www.ingramcontent.com/pod-product-compliance
Lightning Source LLC
Chambersburg PA
CBHW051145190726
48290CB00006B/2002